What the critics are saying…

5 Angels "Shift of Fate is an engrossing, sensual read. The sex is hot and exciting while the story line moves at an excellent pace. Elisa Adams ingeniously describes the ecstasy that can be found in the arms of someone you can trust completely. I could not put the book down and I did not want the story to end. I hope Elisa Adams writes more about Royce, Merida, and Wil. Her Vampires are quite alluring." *~ Dena for Fallen Angel Reviews*

"Shift of Fate is a story of the supernatural with plenty of suspense and romance. Readers are sure to enjoy this spine tingling tale by Elisa Adams." *~ Christy Hayes for eCataromance*

5 Flames "This story is HOT HOT HOT! The love scenes are scorching. You will need a bottle of water nearby. You are hooked at page one and it won't let you go until the very end. The romance between Royce and Merida will keep you entertained as they both try to fight what they feel for each other. Get this one!" *~ Jenni for Sizzling Romances*

Elisa Adams

Shift of Fate

DARK PROMISES

ELLORA'S CAVE
ROMANTICA PUBLISHING

An Ellora's Cave Romantica Publication

www.ellorascave.com

Dark Promises: Shift of Fate

ISBN # 1419951203
ALL RIGHTS RESERVED.
Dark Promises: Shift of Fate Copyright© 2004 Elisa Adams
Edited by: Martha Punches
Cover art by: Syneca

Electronic book Publication: June, 2004
Trade paperback Publication: August, 2005

Excerpt from *Just Another Night* Copyright © Elisa Adams, 2002

Warning:

The following material contains graphic sexual content meant for mature readers. *Shift of Fate* has been rated *E-rotic* by a minimum of three independent reviewers.

Ellora's Cave Publishing offers three levels of Romantica™ reading entertainment: S (S-ensuous), E (E-rotic), and X (X-treme).

S-*ensuous* love scenes are explicit and leave nothing to the imagination.

E-*rotic* love scenes are explicit, leave nothing to the imagination, and are high in volume per the overall word count. In addition, some E-rated titles might contain fantasy material that some readers find objectionable, such as bondage, submission, same sex encounters, forced seductions, etc. E-rated titles are the most graphic titles we carry; it is common, for instance, for an author to use words such as "fucking", "cock", "pussy", etc., within their work of literature.

X-*treme* titles differ from E-rated titles only in plot premise and storyline execution. Unlike E-rated titles, stories designated with the letter X tend to contain controversial subject matter not for the faint of heart.

Also by Elisa Adams:

Shift of Fate
Dark Promises

Chapter One

Merida lounged in her favorite chair, her eyes closed, the sounds of the gulls flying overhead and the waves breaking against the shore a hundred feet from the patio surrounding her. The scents of warm saltwater and hot sand filled her senses, the heat of the May sun warming her tanned skin.

She let her eyes drift open and scanned the length of the beach. Not a soul in sight. Just how she liked things. For the first time in her life, she felt completely—and peacefully—alone. No older brother to tell her to behave herself, no domineering boss to tell her what to do...and best of all, no vampires to mess with her head and play havoc with her emotions.

"Can I get you anything before I leave for the day?"

She glanced up at Brett, the housekeeper too sexy for his own good. Okay, so she wasn't *that* alone. He stood over her chair with his feet apart. The way he had his hands clasped behind his back pulled his emerald green shirt tight against his well-built chest. Brett was muscular, but not overly so, like a certain vampire she knew, with chocolate-brown hair and eyes, and features too smooth to be called rugged. Her brother's mate had called him "pretty" the last time she'd visited, and Merida had to agree. The description fit. She'd never asked, but he couldn't be more than twenty-one or twenty-two. A baby. But old enough to take to bed—which seemed to be why everyone thought she kept him around.

She didn't.

She'd considered it—she'd have been a fool not to—and he'd proved time and again to be ready and willing, but she couldn't bring herself to go through with it. Her mind refused to look past a certain man she'd rather forget.

"No, thanks. I'm all set. I'll see you tomorrow?"

"Are you sure?" He raised an eyebrow as he spoke, his tone laced with innuendo. If he knew how old she really was—or *what* she was—he'd run as fast as he could in the other direction.

She opened her mouth to accept what he offered, but her mind wouldn't let her answer. She sighed. "Sorry. Not tonight."

"Okay." He gave her a killer smile, one that would have had her doing anything he wanted if she'd been a few centuries younger. "Maybe another time?"

"Definitely."

His smile widened. "Cool. Remember I have an early class tomorrow morning so I won't be able to get here until a little after noon. I can stay late, though, if you'd like."

She resisted the urge to groan in frustration. She had an amazing man right next to her, offering her something she should want, and she couldn't take him up on the offer. "Maybe. We'll see what happens."

"Okay. See ya later." He hesitated for a few seconds before walking toward the gate that led to the front of the house. She stared at his fine ass as he walked away, half wanting to call him back. But she let him go, as she did every afternoon, and regretted the moment she'd introduced herself to Royce Cardoso.

"Damned vampires," she muttered. "Always going and messing everything up."

If she could go back in time to when she'd first met him, that night almost a year ago in a small New England town, she'd change everything. She never would have announced her presence to him. She would have let him walk by, never knowing he wasn't alone in his hunt for the killer they'd been searching. But, on impulse, she'd stepped out of the shadows and offered to help him look. At the time, it had seemed like a good idea. They were both working toward the same goal, so why not work together? She hadn't expected the chemistry that had caused an explosion between them. The one night they'd spent together had been one of the things to cause her to flee to Florida and the solitude of a private estate.

But there were other, deeper reasons, ones that kept her awake at night. If she could stay here for the rest of her life, maybe she'd be able to forget all that had happened.

Not likely.

She'd been in Key West for three months, and images of her old life still haunted her at night with the world quiet and sleeping around her. She drew a deep breath and pushed her sunglasses up her nose. Nothing would ever be the same, and she needed to get used to it. Florida seemed the perfect place to start over. She had all the heat and sun she wanted, all the time, a private beach attached to the mansion she'd purchased, and plenty of space and privacy. Life was sweet. Except...

She shook her head, not willing to go there, not yet. She'd left behind everything she'd known when she'd left New England—her home, her family—she wouldn't put herself through the hurt of thinking about it again. Not when it still felt so fresh in her mind. If Sam had just fired her after that last little mishap, she might have been able to handle it. But he'd gone and dumped a whole bunch of unwanted responsibility on her shoulders.

She wouldn't bow down to what he wanted, what he'd asked of her. She didn't want it, never had, and she wouldn't let him get away with pushing her into a job she had no interest in assuming. So she'd packed her things and moved away. In time, she'd forget her anger and contact Sam, but not now. It was too soon after the confession that had changed her life, and she had more important things to do than worry about his feelings.

Like deny her destiny.

Sam's voice floated through her mind, lingering as it had for so many nights. "Fate is too important to ignore, Merida. You have to accept what you are, and what you're destined to be. You can't fight it."

"Bullshit," she muttered. "The ability of denial is my biggest asset."

The cordless phone on the small metal table next to her chirped, dragging her from depressing thoughts. She snatched the phone up and answered it, hoping against her better judgment that *he'd* finally decided to call.

She let out a sigh when she heard her brother's voice. "Hey, sis."

"Eric."

"Nice to talk to you, too." His tone mirrored all the anxiety and irritation she felt, but for much different reasons. On his last visit, Eric had told her he thought she needed to get professional help. She hadn't been very nice in her reply.

"I'm sorry for snapping. I thought you were someone else."

"Sam? Or Royce?"

She almost blurted Royce's name, but she held it back. No sense giving Eric any more ammunition to taunt her than he already had. "Neither."

"What is it with you?" he asked, his tone reprimanding. "Why are you obsessed with a vampire? He's not a nice guy, Merida. I thought you would have realized that by now."

She nearly laughed. Eric didn't know half of what had gone on between them. If he had, he might have done something ridiculously outdated like try to defend her honor. "Don't you think I know that?" She blew out a harsh breath, trying to keep from yelling at her brother. Hadn't she made it perfectly clear that she wanted no more interference in her life?

"Then why even bother thinking about him? I don't get it."

"That's the beauty of it all. You don't have to. It's *my* life, Eric, not yours and not Sam's. I wish you would stop trying to pressure me, because nothing you say is going to have any effect. I'm capable of taking care of myself. Why don't you go back to playing house with Ellie and leave me alone?"

"Easy, honey. I'm just trying to understand what's going on with you."

Some of her anger deflated at his worried tone. She drew a breath and let it out on a long sigh. "Nothing's going on with me. Nothing at all. I just needed a break. This has nothing to do with Royce."

Yeah, right.

"Yeah, sure it doesn't." Eric's answer echoed the voice in her head, and she could almost feel his tension through the telephone lines. Although they'd formed an alliance of sorts during their hunt for the killer that nearly taken Ellie's life, Eric and Royce couldn't stand each other.

To tell the truth, she and Royce didn't exactly get along, either. She'd never be able to call the man a friend. Every time they got close to one another, they'd been ready to tear each other apart. There had been an intense need under all the animosity…which she promised herself she'd never think about again. End of discussion. "Really, Eric, I couldn't care less about Royce. I've moved on. I'm happy here. You and Ellie should visit, come see the pool I had put in. You'll love it."

"Sounds nice. I'll talk to Ellie. I'm sure she'd love to come down for a visit." She heard the smile in his voice when he spoke again. "I'm glad you're all right. Behave yourself, okay? Don't get into any trouble."

"I never do."

"Sure. You're a perfect angel."

She laughed at his playfully sarcastic tone. Growing up, trouble had seemed to follow her around. Not that she'd done anything to avoid it. Some things never changed. "An angel, huh? What fun would that be? The way I remember it, you aren't exactly up for sainthood yourself."

"Don't remind me. Just don't do anything I wouldn't do."

"That leaves me a lot to play with. Tell Ellie I said hello." She disconnected the call and stood up from the chair, walking to the edge of the patio to bury her toes in the hot sand. She might be able to forget about the secrets Sam had kept from her, but what had happened with Royce would be difficult. Some things were impossible to forget.

* * * * *

Women.

Everywhere he went, they only caused trouble.

Royce slammed the car door and made his way up the three flights of stairs to his tiny walkup apartment. He let himself in and shut the door behind him, walking away before he put his fist through the plaster on the wall next to the door. He didn't want to have to explain another gaping hole in the wall to his landlord — who hadn't been thrilled with the first two.

He grabbed a bottle of water out of the fridge and took a long swallow. He didn't need woman troubles now. In fact, he'd be happy to never have them again. Ever. Since Merida had walked out on him nearly a year earlier, he'd reaffirmed his vow to keep himself at a distance from any and all women. He'd been burned twice. Badly. He refused to let it happen again.

What had happened tonight had been a very different problem, but still he blamed the woman involved. Since coming back from South Africa a few months ago, he'd been working as a private investigator, hoping the change of pace would rid his gut of the insatiable gnawing that had settled too long ago to remember. He'd gone past boredom into apathy a few months ago and had decided a career change might help. Instead, he'd only gotten aggravation. Cheating spouses, insurance fraud…every case sunk him deeper and deeper into his rut. And tonight, when the woman he'd been investigating for her husband broke the back window of his car with a tire iron, he'd been ready to kill.

The time had come for more drastic measures. He had a friend up north, living somewhere in rural Vermont, that he might go visit. He hadn't seen Wil in a while, not since his wilder days years ago. A trip to Vermont to relax and leave worries about work or women behind might be just what he needed. Maybe it would finally help him forget about Merida and how she'd left him—and how angry the whole thing made him. He did *not* like being the one left alone in the morning.

He and Merida had never promised each other more than one night. But he'd hoped—no. Hope was a ridiculous thing. He would be better off forgetting any of it had ever happened. He should just chalk it up to a night of amazing, incredible sex and be done with it. After all, isn't that what he did best? Love 'em and leave 'em—that was him. The description fit perfectly. Any of the women he'd been with since his wife would say the same thing. And in the years he'd lived, that added up to hundreds of testimonials.

So why had Merida been the only one running away?

He abandoned the water for something a little stronger—the bottle of aged red wine his brother had sent to him a few weeks ago. Not bothering with a glass, he took a healthy swig, closing his eyes as the liquid scorched his throat on the way down. Marco often asked him why he tortured himself like this. He hadn't minded giving up most of his human life when he'd become a vampire, but there were some things a man just couldn't give up.

After a few more swigs, he corked the bottle and set it back in the cabinet. With his heightened senses and lowered resistance to alcohol, the wine would hit him hard and fast. He scrubbed a hand down his face as he walked down the hall to his bedroom. The sun would be up soon and, now that the adrenaline rush had started to subside, he felt the weariness of the night weigh down on him. He needed some rest before he did something stupid and barbaric he'd regret later.

He stripped out of his jeans and t-shirt and dropped onto the unmade bed, pulling the sheet up to his waist. The cool sheets felt good against his back, the silence of the room a refreshing change after dealing with another night of busy city streets.

The doorbell rang as he'd started to doze off. The only person he could think of who might visit at this hour would be his brother—and only if there was trouble. His heart pounding, he got out of bed, not bothering to put anything over his boxers before he went to answer the door. To his surprise, he didn't find Marco standing on the other side of the door.

A woman he'd had a fling with a couple weeks back stood in the hallway, an anxious smile on her face. "Hi, Royce."

"Hi." He leaned a hip against the doorframe, wondering what this one wanted. They always wanted something, and she—what was her name again?—would be no exception.

"I hadn't heard from you in a while."

He crossed his arms over his chest and frowned at her. He'd never made any kind of a commitment with her, and he'd been ready to go his own way after just a few…dates. "I've been busy."

"I figured. Can I come in?"

"That depends. What brings you by so early in the morning?"

"I knew you'd be just getting in. I thought you might

be lonely."

He raised an eyebrow. "So you came to keep me company?"

"Yes." Her gaze drifted to his boxers before coming back up to his face. "If you're *up* for it."

He swung the door open wider and moved to the side, allowing her to step past him into the apartment. She thought he might be lonely. Huh. She had no idea how true that was.

Chapter Two

"What the hell…?" Wil Brogan let his whispered voice trail off as he took in the sight in front of him, something akin to a scene out of a slasher flick. In ten years on the Caswell police force, he'd never come across anything quite like this. *Not here.* He'd seen it—and worse—but in another life, another time.

A time he'd tried hard to forget.

He stepped further into the room, his gaze landing on the handful of officers standing around the bodies. "Is this how they were found? Just like this?" Back in New York, he wouldn't have even had to ask the question. But in Caswell, all bets were off. The officers went through all the training on how to handle crime scenes, but the most they ever dealt with all the way up in Vermont might be an accident caused by reckless or drunk driving. Murder…the town hadn't seen anything like this in all the years he'd lived here. Most—if not all—the officers on the force had never seen something so gruesome.

Wil had. Many, many times. He kept the memories stored in a place he no longer cared to acknowledge. The sight in front of him dragged the memories from the deepest recesses of his mind, twisting his gut into a painful knot and making his head pound.

One officer, Ray Denton, ran a chubby hand down his face, his eyes reflecting the same torment and horror Wil felt inside—but for very different reasons. "Yeah. Nobody's moved them. Ms. Henderson walked in and found them just like that."

Wil swung his gaze toward the kitchen, where Lora Henderson, a woman who lived down the street half a mile or so, stood talking to another detective. She waved her hands around in nervous gestures as she spoke, her pale face stained with tears. He'd be willing to bet she'd see the bodies in her nightmares for years to come.

He let out a harsh breath as he paced the length of the room, his mind stuck in a past he no longer claimed as his own. Before the memories drove him mad, he turned his focus back to the task at hand—the bloody crime scene spread out before him.

"This is *exactly* how the room was found? Nobody's touched *anything*, right?"

Denton shook his head, his eyes barely concealing his apparent annoyance at Wil's questioning. "Nothing has been touched in the time I've been here, since the call first came in."

Good. The last thing he needed, on top of this mess, was an argument with the crotchety old medical examiner. Wil pinched the bridge of his nose and closed his eyes. The coppery tang of blood filled the air—and his senses—making his stomach churn. He also detected a faint odor similar to burnt hair, though he doubted anyone else in the room had noticed. He was thankful for that, knowing it would cause too many questions. Knives—what would probably be determined as the murder weapon—didn't burn. He knew of a few other things that would cause a burning smell, none of them within the realm of believability for the people of Caswell.

He snapped his eyes open and once again scanned the dim room, lit by a couple of table lamps and the small streams of moonlight filtering in through parted curtains. He doubted the lighting seemed even adequate to those around him—yet he had no problem taking in every minute detail.

One—a man—lay on his back on the floor, arms and legs spread at odd angles. His throat was slashed...no, not slashed. His throat had been *torn out*, his light-colored shirt stained with blood and ripped in several places. Wil shuddered. At first glance, he couldn't make out where the torn shirt ended and the ripped skin began.

The body of a woman lay nearby, sprawled half on the couch and half on the floor. Her dark hair glistened with what could only be blood, her only visible injury a gash over her right temple. Nausea swept over him and he leaned against the nearest wall, covering his mouth and nose with his hand and drawing a deep breath. He'd skipped one too many meals and slept too few hours in the past couple of days to be handling a murder investigation. Especially one this bloody.

A thousand questions raced through his mind, but he didn't have a single answer. What had happened in this apartment? Something about it felt...off. He blew out a frustrated, disgusted breath. He had a sick suspicion that some very, very bad shit had only just begun. Something the little town PD wouldn't be able to handle on its own.

"Wil?"

He heard Michelle's voice from somewhere behind him and spun to find her standing in the open doorway, a brown grocery sack clutched in her hands. He met her questioning, nervous gaze with a slight shake of his head. "Go home," he mouthed to her. It didn't surprise him when she didn't budge.

He stalked across the open-concept living room and kitchen area to the door where she stood. "What are you doing here?"

She looked up at him and blinked a few times, her cheeks red. "I just got home from work. I saw the police cars outside and then this…" She gestured to the house behind him. "What's going on? Is someone hurt?"

He centered himself in the door, blocking the crime scene from her eyes as best as he could. "Yeah. It's…" He locked his gaze with hers, trying to figure out if he spoke to Michelle the woman he had dated on occasion, or Michelle the newspaper reporter who would give anything for a good story. Unable to make the determination, he shook his head. "This is a crime scene, so you're going to have to leave."

He tried to back her out of the room, all thoughts now centered on protecting the integrity of the crime scene. Not that it really mattered—they wouldn't to find the killer. At least not by human investigative means.

She smoothed back a few strands of dark, wavy hair as she stared at him. Her red lips parted and her face drained of all color. "Are Nick and Lisa okay? Is someone hurt? Wil, please tell me what's going on."

For a moment, he let himself feel bad for her. She shared a duplex with these people, probably saw them every day. But then he thought back to the last conversation they'd had and reality set in. He hardened his gaze and crossed his arms over his chest. "I'm working here. Since you're *not*, I suggest go home and put your groceries away before they spoil."

She raised an eyebrow at him and stood her ground. "I'm not leaving until you tell me what's going on. I live next door, Wil. I think I have a right to know."

He cursed under his breath. He didn't need this. He had a job to do, and he didn't need her getting in the way of him running things by the book—as much as he could with an unusual case like this. "Listen well, because I'm only going to say this once," he told her, his voice low and menacing. "Two people are dead in here. I've got to deal with this. You march your little ass over to your side of the house, go inside, and close and lock the door behind you. If I see you out here one more time tonight, I'm going to lock you up for getting in the way of an investigation. Do I make myself clear enough or do you need me to demonstrate?"

"Two people are dead? That's terrible." She tried to glance around him and look in on the scene, and Wil knew she wouldn't forget anything. He had a feeling none of her sudden concern had to do with worrying about friends. Michelle planned to write a book. She'd confessed the whole story to him the last time they went out—including how she wasn't above using people to get the facts she needed for a good story. She'd been looking for the right plot—full of excitement and violence. Things she said the American public ate up. With his luck, she'd probably see this crime as her perfect opportunity.

Not if he could help it. He took a step toward her. "I mean it, Michelle. Go home or I'm going to have to arrest you."

She looked at him, her expression a mix of disbelief and anger. "You wouldn't dare arrest me. I'm worried about my neighbors, who are most likely dead from what you've told me. Is that okay with you?"

He snorted. "Worry? Don't lie to me, or yourself. You're just in it for the story, and we both know it. That's your traditional M.O., using situations—and people—to get what you want."

She shot him a frosty glare. "What's that supposed to mean?"

"I know why you were with me, and it wasn't for who I am as a person. It had a lot more to do with my job, and the resources it would provide you."

She had the decency to look affronted, but even that was an act. Her eyes betrayed the coldness inside her. "I would never use you like that."

And rats didn't squeak. "How stupid do you think I am?"

She lowered her eyelids, gazing toward the ground. "I'm sorry if that's the impression you got. I'm also sorry I disturbed you at work. I'll go home now and let you get back to your job." She glanced back up at him, a hopeful glint in her eyes. "Maybe you can stop by later, when you're done here? This is shocking, and I could really use the company."

"Not now, Michelle. In fact, not ever again. Go home, or I'm going to lock you in a squad car until all of this is done."

He walked away from her before he said or did something he'd regret later. His blood boiled and his head pounded even worse. What had he ever seen in her? He was getting too old for this. Way too old, and way too tired of the bullshit.

He pushed the whole situation out of his mind so he could put his focus where it really belonged—the crime scene. He'd have a long road ahead of him trying to solve this case, and he didn't think he'd be able to go it alone. He'd need to bring in some outside help just to sort through all the clues none of the other officers would pick up. Thankfully, he had an old friend who wouldn't mind doing him a favor or two, provided he didn't catch the guy at a bad time.

Chapter Three

The telephone startled Royce out of a deep sleep. He glanced at the glowing red numbers on the clock on the nightstand, the only light in the otherwise pitch-black room. Nine p.m. He'd overslept again. Groaning, he rolled over and fumbled for the phone receiver, finally managing to bring it to his ear. "What?" he whispered, rubbing his face with his free hand.

He heard a familiar voice on the line. "Did I wake you up?"

"Wil Brogan?" Awakening a little more, he sat up in bed. "It's been a long time."

"Yeah, it has."

Royce raised an eyebrow at the strained tone of Wil's voice. "What's going on?"

Wil's harsh breath confirmed Royce's suspicions. "I need a little advice."

As Wil explained about the murders in the small town where he lived, the woman in bed next to Royce stirred. She rubbed her warm, nude body against his side. He nudged her away.

"You think it's something other than human?" he asked Wil.

"I know it is. There are some things here inconsistent with human involvement. It's a lot to get into over the phone, but I don't think this thing is going to go away quietly. Can you get away for a few weeks?"

Royce nearly laughed at the prospect. After spending most of the past eight months drifting from place to place, looking for anything to fight the gnawing boredom that had long ago settled in his gut, he'd relish any change of scenery. "Yeah. I'd actually thought about coming up for a visit anyway. I just need a day or two to get things in order here."

The woman in bed with him whispered his name, her soft breath fluttering across his stomach as she spoke. When he didn't answer, she put her hand on his bare thigh and squeezed, her nails digging into his skin. He hissed out a breath and shifted away from her, shutting her out of his mind to focus better on Wil's problem. "You're still in Vermont, right?"

"Yeah."

The woman—Nancy? Nicole?—chose that moment to tug on his leg hairs and clear her throat. "Royce, would you get off the phone and pay attention to me?"

"Hold on, Wil." He placed his hand over the receiver and spoke to her. "Just give me another minute, okay? This is kind of important."

He thought she might have huffed and puffed a little, but he didn't really notice. He turned his attention back to Wil and the situation at hand.

"Look, I've got to get back to work. We'll talk more about it all when you get here," Wil told him.

"See you in a few days." He reached for her when he disconnected the call, but his hands only grabbed a fistful of blanket. She stood in the middle of his floor, pulling on her clothes with jerking motions. He ran a hand through his tangled hair. "Where are you going?"

She didn't even bother to look at him as she started

buttoning her shirt. "I'm going somewhere where I'm noticed and appreciated. Where I don't get ignored."

"Correct me if I'm wrong, but I think I appreciated you all morning, and again all afternoon."

She stopped dressing and blinked at him. "You *appreciated* my body. Do you even remember my name?"

"Uh…"

"Yes, that's what I thought." She zipped her skirt and tucked her shirt into it. "I skipped work for this. The least you can do is remember who I am. Do you know how difficult it was for me to get the day off?"

Not as difficult as it had been for him to stay awake for most of the day when he should have been sleeping. But she wouldn't understand that. "Sure I can't convince you to come back to bed? I'm off the phone for now."

"You've got to be kidding me. I'm not some little tramp you can use when you want sex." She shook her head, her bleached-blonde hair fanning around her shoulders. "I deserve to be treated better than this. All women do."

Hadn't she come to him, looking for sex? If anyone should feel used, it should be him. "What did I do? I told you to wait until I was off the phone. If you'd just given me a second—"

"I gave you more than a second. Was that call really so important that it couldn't wait?" She put her hands on her hips and frowned at him.

"Obviously, or I wouldn't have made you wait." He shook his head. "Why are we fighting over this? Just come back to bed and I'll make it up to you."

She gave him a sad smile. "You don't get it, do you? You're so out of touch with reality that you don't even realize when you hurt people. One of these days, you're going to meet a woman you really care about, and she's going to pretend you don't even exist. Maybe then you'll learn that there's more to this life than pleasing yourself."

He held back a groan. Not the one-woman-for-every-man speech. He'd heard that too many times in his life to count. "Correct me if I'm wrong, but didn't I please you several times today?"

Her cold expression deflated and her shoulders hunched. "Yes, you did. But that isn't the point. I overlooked you calling me by another woman's name in the heat of passion, but if you can't remember my name even now I don't know why I bother to keep seeing you."

A cold chill ran down the back of his neck. "I called you another woman's name?"

"Yes. And just for the record, I'm Noelle, not Merida." Finished dressing, she opened the door and started to leave. She turned back, looking at him with a mixture of contempt and pity in her gaze. "It's time to grow up. You can't go on living like a teenager forever. Goodbye, Royce. Have a nice life."

The door shut with a soft click as she walked out. Her high-heeled shoes clacked on the hardwood floors of his apartment, echoing through the halls. He barely noticed the sound, too caught up in what she'd revealed. He'd called her Merida? *Fuck.* What would he have to do to finally exorcise that woman from his head?

He thought back to what Wil had told him about the strange occurrences in Caswell and an idea hit him. He might be able to get her out from under his skin and help a friend at the same time. He picked the phone back up and dialed his friend Ellie's number.

"Hey, kiddo. It's good to hear your voice," he said when she answered the phone.

"Royce, where have you been? We haven't heard from you in months."

L.A., New York, and Chicago before traveling back to New England and settling in Boston a short time ago—though he hadn't told many people. He just wanted to be left alone. "I've been around. How have you been?"

"You'd know the answer to that question if you'd bothered to call once in a while."

He laughed to himself at Ellie's mothering attitude. Some things never changed. "Is Eric home?"

Ellie hesitated before she answered. "Why do you ask?" Royce couldn't fault her for her response. He and Eric had never pretended to be friends, and he knew Eric didn't like the idea of Royce keeping in contact with Ellie.

"I need to get in touch with his sister. She's not still living near you, is she?"

"No. She's down in Florida. Key West. Last time I spoke to her, she sounded so happy there. She bought a house. I don't think she plans to come back."

Good. The further away she stayed the better. He just needed her for one more job, and then they could both get back to their separate lives. "Do either you or Eric have a number where I can reach her? It's of vital importance, hon."

"Business or personal?"

A little of both. "Strictly business, Ell. I promise."

"Okay, fine. Just don't tell her you got the number from me. Get a piece of paper."

Five minutes later, he listened to the phone ring,

waiting for the voice that never failed to clench his gut into a painful knot.

"Hello?" she answered, sounding as drained as he felt. Could it be that she didn't have the perfect life Ellie had led him to believe?

"Hey, kitty," he spoke softly, trying to keep his tone light despite the tingling that ran through his nerves. The sound of her voice caused lust and annoyance to well inside him in equal parts, despite the time and distance between them.

She stayed silent for so long he thought she'd hung up. "Are you there, Merida?"

"Yes, I'm here." She let out a long, loud breath. "What do you want?"

Couldn't she at least *pretend* to be happy to hear from him? "Can't I call to check up on an old friend?"

"Of course you can. Why don't I hang up so you can call a *friend* and do that?"

He swallowed hard, his free hand clenching into a fist and the blood pounding in his ears. How did she manage to get his temper up within thirty seconds of saying hello to him? "Very funny."

"It's not meant to be. Unless you have a valid reason for calling, I have more important things to do than sit around chatting with a *vampire*."

His chest tightened at her attitude, making him glad she lived miles away. Nothing with her would ever be easy. He'd be better off breaking all contact—but he couldn't. No matter how much he tried to forget her, he couldn't walk away. With any luck, sometime within the next week or so, he'd be able to. "Actually, I do have a reason for calling. I have a proposition for you."

"Excuse me?"

He smiled as he regained the upper hand in the conversation. "A business proposition, kitty. Don't get your panties in a bunch."

His stomach clenched tighter as he said the words. *He'd* like to bunch her panties. Right before he tore them off her body. He moved the phone away from his mouth and took a few deep breaths, closing his eyes against the fresh onslaught of desire. Forget the control he'd just gained. Around her, he had none. He hated it, and relished it at the same time.

Her voice interrupted his thoughts. "Business, huh? Start talking."

He explained all Wil had told him. She remained quiet until he finished, but he knew she wouldn't keep her doubts and questions to herself for long.

She didn't disappoint. "What makes you think it has to do with something other than humans? Humans kill. All the time, Royce. It doesn't sound like such a strange crime to me."

"Except that there are some things that don't fit, like a burnt scent in the room with no evidence of fire."

She didn't respond at first and he heard tapping on the other end of the line. He smiled as he imagined her drumming those long nails on the telephone receiver. "This isn't some kind of twisted ploy to get me into bed, is it?" she asked, her tone exasperated.

He steeled himself against the fierce jolt of lust thinking about her in his bed caused, as well as the anger at her presumptions. "A little full of yourself? We've already been that route. It didn't work. Or do you not remember?"

"Oh, I definitely remember." He heard her light laugh and wondered exactly what about their encounter she remembered. "So this is just about work, huh? Okay, then. I'll come see what's going on. I'm not promising I won't kill you when I find out it's nothing."

Pride wouldn't let him thank her, so he took the defensive approach instead. "It's *not* nothing. Believe me, kitty, I never would have called you if I didn't think this was something that would interest you. Don't bother showing up if you're just going to be a pain in the ass about it."

"No. I'll come. I said I would. You've definitely aroused my curiosity."

"Is that all I've aroused?"

She hesitated before she answered. "No. It's not. I'll let you know as soon as I make travel arrangements. You're going to have to pick me up at the airport."

"Fine. I'll talk to you later."

He hung up the phone and flopped back on the mattress, hard and horny and wondering if he'd just made the biggest mistake of his life.

Chapter Four

"So where are you headed?"

Merida glanced at the hefty, balding man in the seat next to her. For hours, he'd slept, snoring noisily and drooling on the lapels of his suit jacket. Now, as the plane started its descent into Burlington, he expected to make conversation? Not likely. "Vermont."

He blinked at her, before he started laughing. "I kinda figured that."

She leaned back in her seat and let her eyelids close, rolling her eyes beneath them. Was this guy for real? Did he really think she'd be talking to him at all if they weren't stuck on an airplane? With her mind focused on possible solutions to Royce's friend's problem, she didn't have time for idle chatter. "I'm visiting a friend."

If she could even call him that. They hadn't parted ways on friendly terms. They might have—if she hadn't been scared and run off. But in the end, she knew she'd done the right thing. It never would have worked out between them. She had no desire to be the timid, accommodating woman he expected, and he'd never be able to live with her strong personality. They'd had one incredible night in bed. Nothing more. The rest of the time they'd spent with each other, she'd wanted to strangle him for his chauvinistic attitude and practiced arrogance. There was more to Royce than what he let the world see, but she didn't have the time or the inclination to go digging below the surface.

"A boyfriend?" the man asked, yanking her from her thoughts.

She opened her eyes and glared at him. "Yes."

The man blinked hard, his eyes widening as he turned his attention to a magazine he pulled out of the seat pocket in front of him. She bit her lip to hold back a laugh, glad she didn't have to use stronger methods than a glare to dissuade his attentions. He left her alone as the plane landed and taxied to the gate. As soon as they were able to disembark, he gave her a wilting look, grabbed his carry-on bag, and took off down the aisle.

"Good riddance," she mumbled as she picked up her own bag and followed toward the gateway.

Unease twisted her insides as she thought about seeing Royce again. Working with him wouldn't be easy—she had too many emotions tied up in it. She didn't know why she'd accepted his offer, when she could have easily passed it off to her brother, or anyone else without such a high emotional stake in the situation. But she hadn't. She'd accepted an offer she suspected hadn't been made with solely business in mind, and now she had to deal with the consequences.

She made her way through the terminal to the baggage claim area, where she'd agreed to meet Royce. Pushing through the throng of people waiting for their luggage, she finally located her single black suitcase and pulled it off the moving belt. She scanned the crowd for a big, obnoxious vampire, but only found anonymous obnoxious humans. Had he changed his mind? It would be just her luck to be stuck in Vermont. She started walking toward the glass doors that led outside—and then she saw him and her heart thudded to a stop in her chest. Did any man have a right to be so damned sexy?

"The man is a jerk. A sexy jerk," she muttered to herself as she walked across the carpet toward the door. "But still…a jerk is a jerk, no matter how enticing the package."

A shiver ran through her as she remembered how enticing his *package* really was.

He stood just outside the glass doors, leaning against a cement support beam, his hands in the pockets of his black cargo pants. A long-sleeved black shirt at least a size too small stretched across his big chest and shoulders. Her mouth watered and she had to force herself to keep walking in his direction. The visual stunned her, as it had every time before. He looked just as she remembered—but something seemed different.

She realized what it was when she stepped out of the terminal and into the noisy pick-up area outside. He'd cut his hair. His dark blond locks, which before had been long enough to brush the center of his back, now didn't even touch his shoulders. The cut was short and a little mussed, left long enough on top for a few locks to hang to his eyebrows. It made him look younger, more dangerous, and utterly amazing.

His icy blue gaze snagged hers, telling her he knew what she'd been thinking. One corner of his mouth lifted in a half-smile as she approached and she had to look away to keep from stumbling. She stopped in front of him, trying her hardest to remain in control of her willpower. The things she wanted to do to him…she brushed the thoughts off with a groan. He didn't say a word, just arched a single blond brow and snorted.

"Good to see you, too, Cardoso."

The corners of his eyes crinkled as his smile widened.

"You look...tan."

She glanced down at her sun-browned arms, bared to her shoulders thanks to her sleeveless red t-shirt. "Spending hours upon hours in the sun will do that to a person. Oh, wait. You wouldn't know that, would you? I was beginning to wonder—I mean *hope*—you'd lost your voice."

"You're not that lucky, kitty." He bent to take her suitcase from her but she yanked it out of his reach. She didn't need a man to do anything for her, let alone carry a little bag or two.

"I've got this."

He paused and frowned at her, amusement sparkling just beneath the annoyance in his gaze. "Do you have something in here you don't want me to see?"

"No. I can handle my own bags. I can take down a three hundred pound man without breaking a sweat. I think I can manage a couple of little bags."

"Suit yourself." He pushed himself off the support beam and walked away, leaving her to stand there or follow. As much as she wanted to walk back into the terminal and get on a plane back to Florida, she hurried after him.

No way in hell would she let that infuriating man get the last word.

* * * * *

Merida tapped her fingernails on the center console, watching the scenery flash by out the passenger side window in Royce's car. The moon lit the quiet country roads and stars filled the sky. Hardly any other cars were on the road, and it seemed like they had the night to themselves. Too bad he couldn't even be bothered to speak to her. In the hour they'd been in the car, he hadn't said a word. He hadn't even looked at her, let alone speak to her, and the music he chose to play on the radio gave her a headache. She drew a deep breath, her lungs filling with the clean, masculine scent that made her panties damp. She'd been wound tight since she'd first seen him again and she had to fight to keep from snapping.

She glanced at him, taking in the strong lines of his profile. She wanted to run her finger along the stubble lining his jaw. "So, what have you been up to?"

He didn't even look at her when he responded. "You know. The usual."

As if the man *had* a usual. She narrowed her eyes. Would it kill him to speak civilly to her? How did he expect them to work together when he wouldn't even look at her? Sick of his silent treatment, she clenched her hands and glared at him. "So, what? You've been sleeping with a different woman every night, walking away before sunup, moving from place to place so you don't have to worry about getting close to anyone. Putting down anyone who isn't up to your insanely high standards?"

She expected some kind of denial, or even anger, but his actions took her by surprise. He pulled the car over to the side of the rural road and slammed it into park. She blinked a few times when he turned his icy gaze on her.

"What's all that supposed to mean?"

Thick tension radiated from him, almost a tangible thing in the charged air. If she didn't backpedal…well, she didn't even want to think about what his reaction might be. She was strong, and perfectly capable of taking care of herself, but she didn't doubt they were equally matched in the strength department. "Relax. I wasn't trying to insult you."

He shook his head, a humorless smile forming on his lips. "Yes, you were. You think you know me? Kitty cat, you have no idea who I really am."

Oh, boy. She took a deep breath, her own energy feeding off the anger he emitted. Her body tensed for the fight she felt in the air, her breath coming in quick gasps and her muscles tightening. A *Panthicenos* threatened wasn't a pretty sight—especially a female who spent the better part of her life proving to the men around her she could do anything as well as they could. The man drove her crazy, in so many ways, that she couldn't even think straight around him. She closed her eyes and turned back toward the window, determined not to start something she had no intention of finishing. He didn't seem to want to give her the option to back away.

He grabbed her chin with his big, hot fingers and turned her face back to him. "Unless you know what you're talking about, kitty, I suggest you keep that pretty mouth shut."

She didn't know which offended her more—his domineering attitude or the crack about her mouth. She shoved his hand away, anger spiking inside her. "*Excuse me.* I would have thought you'd be grateful that I came up here to Nowheresville to help you with this. If you can't handle my being here, I suggest you take me right back to the airport. I'd be glad to get the first plane back to Florida and continue my life without the interference of annoying vampires who—"

"Shut up for a second, will you? You're driving me crazy." He didn't give her a chance to react, let alone object, before he crushed her lips with his own.

Any thought of pushing him away fled as he traced the seam of her lips with his tongue and pushed his way inside. She braced her hands against his shoulders, digging her nails into his shirt. As much as she couldn't stand him, she couldn't deny the powerful physical attraction between them. Even after nearly a year's separation, it hadn't diminished an ounce.

His hand came to the back of her neck and his fingers tangled in her hair. A shiver skimmed the length of her spine. Her panties dampened from just the touch of his mouth. It didn't help that she knew exactly how well they fit together, at least in the physical sense. His big hand rested on her thigh, nudging her legs apart. Her willpower fading fast, she let them open and held tighter to his shoulders.

His fingers brushed her mound through the fabric of her pants and she whimpered. Royce tilted her head back further to deepen the kiss while he strengthened his touch, pressing his fingertips over her clit and circling softly. She moaned. It would be so easy—too easy—to take her clothes off and ride him right in the seat of the car. She wanted that almost as much as she wanted her next breath, but she couldn't let it happen, not if she wanted any hope of retaining her sanity.

She pulled away from him and leaned against the passenger-side door. "What do you think you're doing?"

He slumped into his own seat and slapped his hands down on his thighs as a harsh breath escaped his lips. "I have absolutely no idea. Lack of sleep, probably." He put the car back in drive and pulled away from the side of the road without any more explanation.

She stole a glance at him out of the corner of her eye, taking in his reddened face, set jaw, and tense shoulders. Her gaze dropped to his lap and the huge bulge of his erection against the front of his pants. She licked her lips. The chemistry between them shook him as much as it shook her. She still didn't like it, but at least she wouldn't be the only one stuck with it for the days to come.

* * * * *

A half hour or so after his little explosion, Royce pulled his car into Wil's driveway and killed the engine. If he thought the tension between them had been bad before he'd stupidly kissed her…it didn't even compare to the choking pressure now filling the car. "We're here," he told her. He opened the car door and sucked in a deep breath of air untainted with the scent of the ocean warm female that wrapped around Merida. "Do you need me to carry anything for you?"

She got out of the car and slammed the door, rolling her eyes as she opened the back door and got her suitcase and duffel bag out of the back seat. "I told you before I'm all set."

He cracked his knuckles to avoid hitting something, like his car, and got his own bag out of the trunk. He came back around the front of the car, his gaze locked on Merida. He'd never seen anything like her in his life, with her auburn hair in wild curls and her green eyes shooting fiery glances. Fierce and soft and sexy and…mad as hell. She looked ready to kill, and he harbored no doubts that he was the object of her wrath. He shouldn't have touched her. Shouldn't have kissed her. But at that point, he hadn't known what else to do to get her to stop talking.

If she hadn't broken the kiss, he wouldn't have stopped. His still-aching cock proved how ready he'd been to thrust inside her—in the car on the side of the road. Now, as he watched her focus her lethal gaze on him, he realized his mistake. He didn't know if she was the type to run away when things heated up or try to murder him in his sleep. Neither choice seemed preferable.

He leaned in and whispered into her ear. "I really appreciate you doing this."

She raised an eyebrow. "No, you don't. You feel entitled to take whatever you want, whenever you want it. Don't give me that appreciation shit."

"Okay, I was going to try to be nice about this, but forget it now." He stepped in front of her, crowding her until she backed up against the car. "Listen up. If I took what I wanted, when I wanted it, kitty, I would have had you bent over the hood of my car, my cock slamming into you, about an hour and a half ago."

Her lips parted and she blinked up at him, surprise in her gaze for all of two seconds before she shoved the bitch mask back into place and scooted around him. "Don't even *think* about it. If you touch me again, with any part of your body, I will do some serious damage to a few of your most prized body parts. I'm not going to warn you again. Now are we going to stand here all night or are we going to go inside so I can meet your so-called friend?"

"Yeah. Fine. Come on." He led her up the winding stone path leading to the farmhouse Wil had made his home for the past ten years. Weeds poked up through the cracks in the walkway and the grass looked like it hadn't been cut in weeks. Merida glanced around and shook her head.

"What's with your friend? He's never heard of a lawnmower?"

"He's got a little problem with sunlight, and the neighbors would probably get mad if he mowed the lawn after dark."

He started to walk up the porch steps, but her hand tugging on the back of his shirt brought him to a halt. "What now?"

"You can't be serious. I'm going to be staying here alone with two vampires?"

He fought the burst of laughter that rose in his chest at her anxious expression. "Don't worry. We only bite when we get hungry."

A chuckle escaped his lips at the fire that flashed in her eyes. He chucked her chin with his thumb and walked up the porch steps to the front door. Wil pulled the door open a few seconds after his knock.

"Hey, man. Good to see you."

Royce smiled at his friend, one of the few he cared to keep. He'd known Wil for years, hundreds of them, and neither of them had changed much during the course of their friendship. "Good to see you, too. It's been a long time."

"Too long," Wil agreed. He glanced around Royce to where Merida stood leaning against the porch railing, a scowl marring her delicate features. "Who's this?"

"This is Merida. She works for Sam Kincaid," he told Wil, mentioning a former boss of Royce's—a man nobody dared mess with.

"She does?"

Royce nodded. "She'll help us out with this. Trust

me."

"She doesn't anymore," Merida mumbled. "You would have known that, vampire, if you'd bothered to ask. And how about not talking about me like I'm not right behind you, okay?"

"Whatever you say, dear." Royce laughed and shook his head, turning his attention back to Wil. "She does this kind of thing for a living. Don't let her claws scare you, though. She's all talk. Well, mostly anyway."

Wil didn't look too sure, but he opened the door and let them both inside. He glanced at Merida with an uncomfortable expression on his face. "Can I get you something to drink?"

Royce watched Merida, trying to gauge her reaction to Wil. His size, along with his dark eyes and hair, intimidated a lot of people. Merida didn't look intimidated, though. She looked bored.

She shook her head at Wil's offer. "As much as I'd like to sit around chatting all night, I've got to get some sleep. You know us night sleepers. Always putting a damper on the party. Do you have a couch or something I can camp out on for the night?"

Wil looked at Royce with a questioning expression. Instead of strangling her for her attitude like he really wanted, he just shrugged. Wil rolled his eyes. "I've got a couple of spare bedrooms. Unless you two want to share?" He glanced from Royce to Merida and back again.

Merida's eyes widened and her jaw dropped. "No. Absolutely not. If you've got the extra room, I'd rather have my own bed. Otherwise I can go sleep in the car."

Wil shot Royce an amused look before returning his attention to Merida. "No problem. I have plenty of room.

Follow me." He led her toward the stairs.

"Goodnight, kitty," Royce called after her. She didn't even acknowledge his comment as she followed Wil upstairs and out of sight.

Royce had settled himself onto the blue denim couch by the time Wil came back downstairs five minutes later. He turned his accusing gaze toward Royce. "Why did you bring her here?"

"I thought she might be able to help us out."

"A human, Royce? In the middle of this? Are you nuts?" Wil flopped down on the couch next to him and rested his elbows on his thighs.

Royce laughed at Wil's assumption. "She isn't human. She's *Panthicenos*, and she knows what she's doing. She's been doing this kind of stuff longer than I've been alive."

Wil sat back and whistled long and low. "*Panthicenos*, huh? A little thing like that? I never would have guessed. She doesn't like you very much, though, does she?"

"Not at the moment." He shrugged a shoulder. "Give me time. I'll get back in her good graces again."

Wil leaned back against the couch, propping his feet up on the coffee table. "What did you do, sleep with her and leave her?"

He wished. "No. Actually, it was the other way around."

"You're kidding me."

Royce kicked at a loose leg on the coffee table, wanting somehow to get the cat out of his mind. "I wish. I don't want to talk about Merida now, okay? I just want to forget, at least for the night, that she's here."

"I don't know how you could."

Royce glanced up at Wil's appreciative tone, narrowing his eyes at his friend. "Keep your hands off her."

"Wouldn't dream of laying even one finger on her, buddy." A slow, knowing smile spread over Wil's face. "Not if she's yours. But if the two of you aren't involved, it seems to me like she'd be fair game."

Somehow, he didn't think Merida would appreciate being referred to as game. But he'd let Wil find that one out on his own. "Hands to yourself, Brogan, okay?"

"Sure. I wouldn't touch what belongs to someone else. You know me better than that."

Yeah. That's exactly what Royce was afraid of.

Chapter Five

Sunlight streaming through the parted curtains woke Merida early the next morning. She dragged herself out of bed, grabbed some clothes, and walked to the bathroom for a quick shower. She passed two closed doors on her way, presumably the day sleepers already at rest. She breathed a sigh of relief that she wouldn't have to deal with their irritating egos until after the sun went down. She had the day to herself. And she'd need the time to think. Being back in New England brought unwanted memories to the forefront of her mind.

Once showered and dressed in jeans and a cropped black t-shirt, she pulled her still-damp hair back into a loose ponytail. She put on her shoes and went outside, sitting on a bench in the corner of the wraparound porch. The quiet solitude of the morning comforted her. A light breeze rustled in the branches of the trees surrounding the house. She squinted into the sun-filled yard as a cat ran across the grass. The animal most likely had nothing better to do all day than chase mice and nap. Must be nice to have such a simple life.

Her palms itched and she wriggled her fingers. The longer she sat, the more she wished she had someone to talk to. Anyone. But there wasn't anyone in her life she could trust with her secrets. Living a solitary life, at least emotionally, magic had become her only outlet. Since early childhood, when she'd learned what she was truly capable of, it had been the one thing to keep her grounded when things got crazy—as they so often did these days.

She crossed her legs on the worn wooden bench and rested her hands on her knees, palms up. Her eyelids dropped closed and she focused all her concentration on summoning the ropes Sam had tried to teach her—something that had been giving her trouble for over a year. Each time she got close to getting the ropes to do what she wanted, they fizzled into blue smoke in the air and she had to start again.

She drew in a deep breath, and another, feeling the familiar tingling start at the base of her fingers. *Yes! Finally.* She'd been killing herself to get it right, bending her mind with practice until she couldn't even think straight, and now all her hard work had started to pay off. She could almost feel the thin threads of energy lifting from her palms, spiraling out into the air around her. Maybe next time she'd even be able to open her eyes. Right now, she wouldn't chance it, or anything else that might break her concentration. Like moving. Or breathing.

A twig snapping in the distance broke her concentration. The tiny threads of what would have been psychic ropes snapped free from the anchors of her fingertips and flew away. She opened her eyes just in time to see them zinging through the air like little balloons that hadn't been tied. One hit the window and fizzled out. The other struck the gray clapboard siding, leaving a tiny burn mark as it disappeared. *Damn it! So close…but still not good enough.*

She'd never be like Sam. Why he thought she could even compare to his abilities was beyond her. Of course, he had a few hundred years more practice on his side—and a lot more patience than she'd ever have. She could accept her shortcomings, and a lack of patience happened to be a major one. It made her good at her job, but it also made her a major bitch when things didn't go her way.

She banged her fists on her legs and fought the urge to scream. She'd never get used to actually having to *work* for anything—at least not anything magical. She had a natural ability toward it, and the ropes should have been no exception. It tormented her to know she couldn't get one simple thing right, even after huge amounts of practice. Maybe she had some kind of mental block against the ropes. She wouldn't be surprised, considering she'd been working on conjuring them when Sam had dumped his news on her.

Her mind drifted back to the previous summer, when everything in her life had gone wrong. It hadn't been long after the demon Aiala had tried to kill her brother and Ellie. Not long after her visit to the town where Eric had been staying, and her...mishap with the vampire. She'd been sitting on her bed at the time, practicing the rope trick Sam tried to teach her—with the same results. Back then, her failures had been worse. The first time she'd let the ropes loose into the air, she'd charred her bedroom curtains. The second time, she'd had to buy a new mattress.

"Give it time. It'll come to you."

She'd snapped her eyes open at the sound of the familiar voice. Sam had stood in the doorway, his arms crossed over his chest and his usual serious expression plastered on a face that would have been handsome if it wasn't so downright scary. She was used to seeing him that way—permanent scowl, jagged scars, and all—so it didn't bother her. But she understood why humans wouldn't want to run into the guy alone at night.

"No, obviously it won't. I've been trying and trying"

"For three weeks." He'd walked into the room and rested a foot on her mattress, leaning his forearms on his leg. "The ropes are tough, Rida. Very tough. I've explained it all to you before. It's going to take a while to learn it. The most important thing to do is to keep trying. Don't give up."

"I've never had to work this hard for anything in my life. Practice? I don't usually have to do that. I should be able to think of the ropes, and have them appear."

He'd laughed—a rarity for him. It did nothing to lighten his brooding expression. "That would be like trying to take a calculus exam without even opening the book. Not everything in life comes easily. Some things are worth the extra work. You have to learn that someday. Up until now, you've had things way to easy. Things are going to change. There are going to be spells a lot harder than psychic ropes, cases a lot harder than minor demons. If you give up now, you'll never reach your full potential."

Icy fingers of suspicion had walked down her spine. She hadn't considered Aiala a *minor* demon. "My *full potential*? Is this some kind of a test?" She'd rolled her eyes at his silence. "Why are you pulling this shit, giving me spells you know I'm not ready for?"

"You're beyond ready. Ready, in this instance, doesn't mean able. What do you really get out of life if everything comes easily? You've become too complacent with the world as you know it. You can accomplish great things, but you have to apply yourself. Do you realize most *Panthicenos* can't even manage half the magic you can?"

She frowned. "I thought it was natural to us all."

"You've been around enough of us to know that isn't true. Have you spent much time with your brother lately?"

Sam shook his head slowly from side to side. "There are few with your potential, Rida. Less than two percent of us are capable as you are. Do you understand what that means?"

She blinked at him, not sure at all of what he was trying to tell her. "I don't think so. Maybe if you stopped talking in riddles, I could follow you."

"You're destined to be a Balance Keeper. As soon as you finish your education and learn the rest of the magic you'll need to carry out the job."

"A Balance Keeper?" She shook her head, sure she'd heard him wrong. "You can't be serious."

"Why do you think I've let you work for me for this long, when you constantly disregard orders? When you put yourself in unnecessary danger and nearly get others killed on *certain* occasions?"

She knew what occasion he spoke of—the one when she and Ellie, along with Ellie's vampire friend, had tried to vanquish a very powerful demon. It hadn't gone as planned, but at least they'd gotten rid of the demon threatening Eric and Ellie. "I don't know. Tell me why you seem to feel compelled to keep me around."

"You are to be groomed to accept a position as a Balance Keeper, only when the time is right."

"I've been around for almost a thousand years. Don't you think you should have told me sooner?"

"No. You weren't ready. I'm not supposed to tell you now. But, with everything that's happened lately, I thought you needed to know."

Her heart had sunk to her stomach, her throat narrowed. "How long have *you* known?"

"For longer than I've known you. Things have a funny

way of working out, don't they?"

The pieces of an ancient puzzle began to slide together in her mind. Sam had taken in Merida and her older brother Eric when, a thousand years ago, their mother had been killed. They'd been children, barely two and twelve years old, and had nowhere else to go. For all these years, she'd thought it had been because of Eric and a friendship he'd formed with Sam's son. "Is that why you raised Eric and me? Was it because of what I'm supposed to be?"

He confirmed her suspicions with a nod of his head. "Yes. I was named to protect you and start your education when the time was right."

"What about Eric? Why did you accept him as well?"

"I had no choice." Sam turned away and walked toward the door. "I couldn't leave him alone. You needed each other. I'd love to talk with you more about the subject, but it will have to wait until later. I have some things to do."

In typical Sam fashion, he had walked out of the room and closed the door behind him, leaving her alone to think about the huge bomb he'd just dropped on her.

A dog barking in the distance brought her back to the present. She leaned her head back against the rough surface of the bench and blew out a breath. That had been the last conversation she'd had with Sam, a man who'd become like a father to her in the years since he'd taken her in. Her opinion of him had shifted, along with her supposed destiny. No longer did she see him as a man she could trust with her life, because he'd taken away life as she knew it. She'd left that day, fled to Florida to get away from a destiny she didn't want.

She knew what a Balance Keeper did. They spent their

entire lives wandering the world, going from one place to another, destroying the greatest evils the planet had ever known. Neither good nor malevolence could ever be allowed to grow stronger than the other, because power could taint even goodness and turn it into something twisted and ugly.

Balance Keeper? Not hardly. She was just a woman who enjoyed playing with magic. She wouldn't give up herself to make sure the rest of the world stayed safe. If humans felt the need to act like idiots and invite evil demons into their presence, then she wouldn't try to stop the morons from being eaten alive. Not that most species of demon were interested in actually eating humans. They weren't. Some preferred souls, or blood like vampires did, but human flesh? She wrinkled her nose. Disgusting.

Being a demon herself, she could attest to the fact that they weren't all hideous beasts. When she looked in the mirror, she saw a normal, very human-like woman.

Most of the time.

And the times when she looked like a giant cat with glowing eyes and sharp teeth and a scaly spine...well, she wasn't *that* scary. And she wasn't really all that big, either, as far as *Panthicenos* went. She most certainly had no interest in taking her teeth to humans. Not unless they pissed her off. She would never actually *eat* anyone, but she got a huge kick out of threatening big, burly men who thought they were so tough until they caught a glimpse of her incisors.

She lifted her hand into the air, sending a flash of blue light toward the porch roof with a flick of her wrist. It bounced off the wood before evaporating in a puff of white smoke. A chunk of a roof board splintered and hurtled down toward her. A flick of her wrist and it vanished into the air, leaving only a puff of thick, black smoke.

What she'd normally consider a stupid cat trick now served to get her even more frustrated. She got everything else Sam had taught without more than a few minutes of practice. She'd mastered fire, lightning, electricity, even a little wind and rain on good days. She'd been moving objects with her mind since she'd hit five years of age and could read thoughts if she tried hard enough.

Why not the goddamned ropes?

She wiggled her fingers against the armrest, watching as her nails grew longer and thinner and razor-sharp—a mix of human-like fingernails and her *Panthicenos* claws— a trick that worked wonders for scaring the life out of a temperamental quarry. She loved her job. Hunting down criminals and killers, both human and not, gave her a rush. She thrived on the adrenaline. But the magic itself had become her passion.

Now, everything had changed. Her passion had become her *responsibility*, her fate. She didn't know if she liked the sound of that. But at this point, she didn't see that she had much choice. A pang of guilt shot through her stomach as she thought about Sam. She hadn't talked to him since the previous summer. She didn't care to accept a life as a Balance Keeper, but she missed her family. She'd been strong not to call in all the time she'd been away, but homesickness made her weak. She pulled her cell phone out of her pocket and dialed Sam's number.

"Hi, Sam," she greeted when he answered.

"How's Florida?" came his terse reply. She knew he was angry, and that she'd disappointed him, but he hadn't left her much choice. He'd brought it upon himself when he'd tried to force her into a service she refused to do.

"I'm in Vermont now, actually."

"So you did meet up with Royce, then?"

She heaved a sigh. How would he know about Royce contacting her? Eric. She'd called him to let him know where she'd be. He must have called Sam. "Yes. I did."

"Don't do anything stupid." The coldness in his tone hit her like a smack in the face. He'd never spoken to her that way before—like an object of disdain instead of the woman he'd raised like a daughter.

"What makes you think I would?"

"You don't have a very good track record with those things."

A tear welled in the corner of her eye. She swiped it away, having no time for foolishness, especially not when Sam would know. She'd lose any credibility she had left. "Don't start. I'm here to work, and I always do my job."

"I suppose you do." Sam hesitated, and she knew he wanted to ask her how she was doing, but he didn't. He wouldn't either. He'd made his utter disappointment in her quite clear the night she'd quit her job and walked away from her old life. "Tell me. What are you working on?"

She drew a deep, shuddering breath before she answered. "A double murder, as far as I know. I don't have many details yet. I plan to go to into town today and ask around about it."

"Just make sure you're subtle. In a small town like that, you don't want to get people suspicious."

"I can handle it myself." As soon as the words were out of her mouth, she regretted snapping at him. But she refused to take the words back. He'd raised her to have pride—and she couldn't let it go.

The tenderness in his reply surprised her. "I know you can. Believe me. I know."

"How are you doing?" she blurted, her heart aching to be back home.

"Your brother misses you."

She closed her eyes, knowing he meant he missed her as well. "I miss you, too," she mumbled, barely loud enough for him to hear.

"I know you no longer wish to work for me, but you know you can call me if you need any help, right?"

She resisted the urge to tell him she wouldn't do anything of the sort. As much as she valued him, she needed to do this on her own. From now on, she needed to do things her way and not rely on someone who might turn on her years down the road. "Of course."

"Keep in touch, okay? Don't wait another year before you call and let me know how you're doing. Oh, and Merida?"

"Yes?"

She heard Sam's sigh before he continued. "Be careful up there, alone with those two vampires. I don't want to see anything happen to you."

"Always." She disconnected the call, feeling worse than she had before she'd picked up the phone. Why had she felt the need to call him? And why had he warned her to be careful, when he knew damned well she was perfectly capable of caring for herself?

She went back inside and, seeing Royce's car keys on the counter, thought of an idea. In need of breakfast and sure the vampire's cabinets were bare, she lifted the keys off the counter and walked back out the door. He wouldn't mind if she borrowed his car, right? It would only be for a little while, and he'd probably sleep right through the whole thing.

She drove down the winding, twisting dirt roads back toward the center of town they'd driven through the night before. She remembered seeing a little coffee shop on the corner — probably a good place for breakfast and information. She walked into the busy restaurant and grabbed one of the handful of empty tables, a small round one in the corner near the window.

She tried to listen to the conversations of the people around her, but with plates and flatware clattering and oldies music blaring on the radio she couldn't make out enough of any conversation to call it useful.

A thin, dark-haired waitress in a faded yellow apron stopped next to the table. "What can I get for you?" She looked like she couldn't be more than twenty. The nametag pinned to the apron read Nancy.

"Coffee. Is it possible to get a cheeseburger this early in the morning?"

Nancy frowned, but yelled over her shoulder to an older man behind the grill. "Sean, can you make a burger?"

He glanced up long enough to nod his head. "No problem."

"Thanks. What can I say? I'm not really into pancakes."

Nancy shrugged. "It's no big deal. We get some strange requests every once in a while. All those trendy diets, I guess." She filled the chipped beige mug in front of

Merida with steaming coffee and set a small metal pitcher of cream on the table. "I'll be back in a few with your food."

Merida brought the mug to her lips and inhaled, drawing in the rich, hot scent of the strong coffee. She took a small sip, drinking it black. For the first time since arriving, she wondered if Royce's friend might be right. She felt a strange presence, settled around the town, an almost eerie quiet. She'd felt something similar in Stone Harbor last summer. It might be just a little bit of paranoia on her part—or there could be something in the town none of the other patrons in the coffee shop would believe. Everything here seemed too perfect, almost surreal. No talk of murders at all, even though it had just happened days ago. It didn't make sense. Wouldn't *someone* still be wondering what had happened to those people?

"Is everything okay?"

She looked up as Nancy set her plate of food in front of her.

"Oh, yeah. Fine."

Nancy smiled. "Can I get you anything else?"

"Actually, I have a question."

"Sure."

"Do you know anything about those murders a couple of days ago?"

Nancy's eyes widened and she glanced over her shoulder. "You're not a reporter or anything, are you?"

"No. I'm a friend of Wil Brogan's."

"Um, okay." Nancy looked around the room, a nervous glint in her eyes, before she slid onto the empty chair across from Merida. "I just have to be quiet. My mother owns the diner, and she doesn't like me gabbing while I work. I don't know much, just what everyone else does. I heard it was horrible, that the bodies were mutilated. At least that's what Michelle told me."

"Michelle?"

"Silverman," Nancy said it like Merida should have known. "You know, Wil's girlfriend."

"Oh, yeah. Her." Either Royce had failed to mention Wil's girlfriend to her, or Wil hadn't bothered telling Royce about her.

"She's a reporter for the *Caswell Gazette*. She thinks it was some kind of cult thing. At least that's what she's telling everyone in town."

"Really?"

Nancy's gaze locked with Merida's. The younger woman seemed to be searching Merida's face for something. When she finally spoke, her tone had lowered even more. "You said you're a friend of Wil's."

"I did."

"Then I think you should know something about him."

The hair on the back of Merida's neck prickled. "What's that?"

"Michelle thinks...oh, never mind. I really shouldn't be telling these kinds of things to a complete stranger."

Merida concentrated, pushing herself into Nancy's mind. *It's okay. I'm safe. I won't tell anyone what you tell me.*

Nancy's eyes widened, but Merida just smiled. *You can trust me, Nancy.*

"Michelle thinks Wil might have something to do with the murders," Nancy blurted.

Shock slammed into Merida. "She what? Why would she think that?"

"You wouldn't believe the stuff Michelle has dug up about him. He left the police department in New York City after a case that went wrong. Michelle said he's got what she described as a shady past and she doesn't know how he even got hired here. And, she said he's been acting strange lately, jittery, like something's wrong."

"Do you talk to Michelle a lot?"

Nancy shrugged. "She comes in a few times a week. Her mother and mine were close friends growing up. Michelle is a few years older than me. She used to baby-sit me and my sisters."

Merida filed away the information she got from Nancy for later, when she could ask Wil about what Michelle had been saying. She wondered if Michelle knew more than she was letting on. Why would she try to implicate a police detective in a double murder? She could just be a reporter hungry for a story, but she might not be, either. Before she came to any conclusions, though, she needed more information.

"How long have she and Wil been together?"

"About four months, but she'd been hounding him a lot longer than that. You've seen the guy. Do you blame her? But he's so hesitant. He's such a recluse, everyone in town has been afraid to approach him. In the ten years he's been around here, I guess he's only made a handful of friends. He's weird, keeps to himself. Honestly, I have to tell you he gives me the creeps. No offense. I know he's your friend and all."

"None taken." So Wil gave everyone the creeps and dated a reporter that may or may not know more about the murder than she was saying. That didn't speak well for his judgment. Or his personality. When Wil woke up later that night, she had a gazillion questions she'd need answered. "Where is this house located?"

"It's at the very end of Magnolia Street. Take a right at the end of Main Street, go a couple of miles down the road, and Magnolia Street will be on the left. It's the door on the left. Michelle's is on the right."

"Wait a second. Michelle lives in the same building?"

Nancy nodded, and Merida moved Michelle a little higher on her suspicion list.

She thanked Nancy for her time and rushed to eat her meal before she paid the bill and left. What Nancy had told her had her curiosity aroused, and she couldn't wait to find out if any of it was true. After a quick stop at the local market for a few necessities—food that didn't come in blood bags—she followed Nancy's directions to the house Wil's girlfriend shared with the murder victims. Until she saw the scene of the crime, she couldn't let herself form any conclusions.

Chapter Six

Merida gave the front door a sharp push. It swung open slowly, with a foreboding creak. She stepped inside, careful to shut the door behind her in case anyone drove by. The house sat in a relatively unsettled area, but she didn't see a point to taking unnecessary chances.

Despite the bright sun shining outside, the interior of the house felt dark and damp—the mark of a nonhuman entity. Merida rubbed her hands up and down her arms to ward off the chill. Her running shoes scuffed along the hardwood floor that ran the length of the huge room that served as a kitchen, dining room, and living room. The scent of dried blood hung heavy in the air, along with the burnt smell Wil had detected. It wasn't strong, but she definitely caught it in the thick, moist air.

Electricity filled the expansive room that set her nerves on edge. Humans were so much easier to take care of than whatever this thing was—probably some kind of demon, but she couldn't put a name to it until she had more facts. For now she filed it away in her mind as a royal pain in the ass.

She spent several hours combing through every room in the house, right down to the half bath in the basement. She found no sign of current demonic presence, but that didn't really mean anything. Certain demons had unusually good cloaking abilities. For all she knew, the killer might be watching her as she watched for it. The thought gave her a chill.

* * * * *

When Royce dragged himself out of bed just after sunset that night, a horrible charred smell filled the entire house. He pulled on a pair of jeans over his boxers and, scrubbing a hand down his face, stumbled down the back stairs to the kitchen and the source of the offensive odor. Merida stood by the stove, back to him, humming to herself as she cooked.

He narrowed his eyes as he stopped behind her. "What the hell are you doing? Do you have any idea how early it is?"

"I'm cooking, obviously. I take no responsibility for your overly sensitive nasal passages." She turned to him, brandishing a huge silver meat fork.

He held his hands up and stepped back, not wanting to lose any vital parts so early in the evening. "Whoa, kitty. Easy with that thing."

She smiled. "What's the matter? Is the big, powerful vampire afraid of a little fork?"

"In your hands, yes. Sometimes I think you're a little unstable."

Instead of laughing at the mock insult, or hurtling one right back as he thought she would, she frowned and turned back to the pan on the stove. Curious. "Did I say something wrong?"

She shook her head, but didn't turn around to look at him.

"Merida?"

When she turned back to him, she had a smile plastered on her face he suspected was about as phony as his insults. She held a large white plate in her hands. "I broiled some steak, and steamed fresh broccoli. Do you want some?"

His stomach churned as he got a whiff of the green vegetable. The steak he could handle if she'd cooked it very rare, but he'd abandoned vegetables too many years ago to count. "What's that smell? It isn't meat or vegetables."

She finally laughed. "The stove hadn't been used in a long time, I guess. There was a little dust on the burners."

A little? The room smelled like she'd exploded a dust rhino. He glanced at the plate she held with mild interest. "That steak looks pretty rare. Do you mind if I have a little?"

She frowned at him. "I was just kidding. I didn't think you ate at all. Not food, at least."

He shrugged. "I don't mind a good steak now and then."

She grabbed a second plate out of the cabinet, cut a large chunk of steak from her piece, and pushed it onto the plate. "Here you go. Um, enjoy." She seemed to be watching him with rapt interest, so he cut a piece off the steak and slipped it into his mouth. He chewed slowly, savoring the flavor of the human food he usually avoided. Once in a great while he missed eating, but his sensitive taste buds couldn't handle the extreme flavor of most food.

Merida kept giving him odd glances in between bites, as if she expected him to keel over and die at any minute. She probably *hoped* he would, but she wasn't that lucky.

"I see you went shopping today," he mentioned, trying to break the tension that had settled over them once again. He swallowed hard, lust slamming into him full-force as her tongue ran over her bottom lip. Still waking up, he couldn't put up defenses fast enough to keep out her scent—a scent that drove him to the brink of sanity. The muscles in his shoulders bunched.

She must have noticed a change in him, because her eyes widened and her lips pursed. He saw shades of the fighter he knew her to be as she braced herself. He let out a slow breath, hoping to keep things civil between them. She'd made it quite clear he didn't interest her, not in the physical sense. But if she kept doing sexy things he couldn't be held responsible for his actions.

"Yes, I went shopping. I also had breakfast downtown and went over to see the house where the murders took place."

She said it so casually he might have missed the last part if he hadn't been listening well enough. "Hold on. You did what?"

"I went to see where those people were killed." She kept eating like she hadn't just confessed to breaking the law. He put down his fork and stared at her.

"Are you nuts? Couldn't you have just waited for Wil?"

She opened her mouth to answer, her eyes flashing fire, when Wil appeared in the kitchen doorway. "Waited for me for what?"

"She went to the crime scene today."

Merida shot him a killer glare and he knew he'd pay for it when they were alone.

Wil sighed. "That probably wasn't the best idea. If someone had caught you, you might have been arrested. Then you would have had to wait until my shift tonight for someone to bail you out."

"You've got to be kidding me. Between the two of you superegos, I don't know who is worse." Merida dropped her fork on her plate and shoved it away.

Wil closed his eyes and pinched the bridge of his nose. When he opened his eyes again, he threw Merida a reprimanding look. "Just wait next time, okay? It's not good for you to be slinking around town, sneaking into places that are off-limits."

Merida rolled her eyes but kept her mouth shut. Wil should count himself lucky for that—though she'd probably take it out on Royce later.

Wil walked over to a mirror hanging just inside the doorway and tied his tie. "I have to work tonight. I tried to get the night off, but the department is shorthanded as it is, and with the murders, everyone is scared. I'll see what I can do about getting out early, before sunrise, and then I'll take you back to the house. I can fill you in on the way the bodies were found, and what information I have."

"Thank you." The way Merida spoke worried Royce. She sounded a little too polite and accommodating. What did she have planned? He'd have to see that she didn't sneak back out of the house without him again. If she got caught and arrested, it wouldn't look good for any of them. Her presence had to be kept quiet, and he didn't like her running around town alone.

He didn't like how she acted so nice to Wil, either. Why did she treat Wil with what seemed to border on respect when she didn't have a nice word for him?

Wil glanced down at the plate in front of Royce and shuddered. "What are you doing?"

"Eating."

"I see that. But why?"

Royce shrugged, his mood rapidly deteriorating. He glanced at Merida with narrowed eyes. She just smiled.

"What did you find out in your travels today?" Wil asked as he sat down in the chair next to Merida.

Royce's hands clenched into fists and he heaved a sigh.

Merida ignored him. "That your girlfriend, the reporter who wants to write a true crime book, lives in the same building where the murders took place and she thinks this is the work of some kind of cult."

Wil's eyes widened and he sputtered. "Where the hell did you find all that out?"

"Nancy at the diner."

"Teenagers." Wil muttered the word like it was a curse. "Yeah, and I suppose you're going to tell me Michelle is right. That humans caused the murder and it has nothing to do with anything out of the ordinary."

"Actually, that's not true." She pushed back from the table and put her half-full plate on the sideboard next to the sink. "I felt an entity there. Definitely not human, and definitely not benign. This guy meant to cause serious trouble, which he did, but I'm not sure if he's done yet. The only thing I don't know is if he's tied to the house, or to a specific person."

"What does that mean?" Wil asked.

She turned and propped her hip on the counter, her arms crossed over her chest. "If he's tied to the house, he won't be able to leave the vicinity. If he's tied to a person, he can go anywhere they go."

"How do we figure out which it is?"

"I'll need to spend more time there, search for a few

more clues. I also need some information on the property the house sits on. Is that the original structure? Have any changes been made to it? Any strange happenings?"

Wil let out a long, harsh breath. "I'll make some phone calls and see what I can find out. Is there anything else we need to do now?"

Merida shrugged. "Don't know yet. For now we just wait and see what happens."

Royce had a feeling there was more to it than that, but she wasn't talking. He decided to let the subject drop. For now. Later, when she'd had time to think about her findings, he'd question her more.

Wil stood, a frown on his face, and ran a hand through his hair. "Okay. I don't like doing nothing, but I guess we don't really have a choice. I've got to go now before I'm late. You," he pointed a finger at Merida, "try and stay put tonight. I'll get whatever information you need and bring it here. And try not to kill each other while I'm gone, okay?" He walked out of the kitchen shaking his head.

Merida turned her back on him again, this time to wash dishes. "What are your plans for tonight?" she asked without looking at him. "I'm assuming you have some things to do?"

Her tone bothered him, but he couldn't figure out why. If he didn't know better, he'd think she might be jealous. A smile formed on his face. Did the fact that he needed to feed bother the little kitty? "Now that you mention it, I do need to go out and find a suitable donor. The steak only made me hungrier, and made me realize I haven't had regular meals lately."

She spun on his, her wet hands on her hips and her

eyes narrowed. "Don't even start. Can't you wait until after I go to bed so I don't have to think about you with some bimbo?"

"Why? Does it bother you that I might go out and find another woman?"

She picked up the dishtowel off the counter, dried her hands, and threw it at him. "Should it? I've been very clear with you from the start. I want nothing to do with you, *vampire.*"

The look in her eyes told him different. She talked big, but she was still as attracted to him as he was to her. When she glared at him, something shifted inside him—a deep, gnawing hunger that had his control slipping a notch. He closed his eyes and blew out a breath. He either had to leave and find food, or convince her to become his next meal. "Nothing to do with me, huh? So you have no interest in volunteering as a donor for the night?"

He snapped his eyes open just in time to see the emphatic shake of her head. "If you think I want that, you're even crazier than I thought. Get the hell out of here before I hurt you."

Hurt sounded like a good thing to his hunger-clouded mind. He advanced a few steps toward her, his fangs elongating as he watched the breath rise and fall in her chest. She was so easy to aggravate, and he had to admit that a little female obstinacy turned him on. He'd never tell her that, but it made him rock-hard every time he saw the spark of anger in her eyes. The hunger inside him grew quickly as he thought about all the times she'd insulted him, given him a taste of her attitude. If she had any idea how goddamned hot it made him, she'd probably never want to argue with him again.

God, he loved a challenge.

His fangs came down fully, the tips biting into his tongue. His breathing became shallow, almost harsh, as he fought for control of something rapidly getting out of hand. He ran both hands through his hair, swiping the shaggy strands back from his forehead. What was wrong with him? Why did he let her affect him this way—and why couldn't he fight the hunger once it started? He'd never known anything like it before. He didn't even feel like himself.

It was his own damned fault for skipping a couple of meals in the last few days. He'd been running on adrenaline alone since the phone call from Wil, and it showed in his lack of composure. But watching the pulse beat in her throat…*shit*.

"So, not willing to be my nightly sacrifice, huh?" he asked, stopping a few inches from her. She squirmed, tried to duck away from him, but it only increased his arousal.

"I don't *think* so," she muttered, but he saw hesitancy flash in her eyes. He'd be willing to bet if he touched her sweet pussy, she'd be damp for him.

His cock tightened against his zipper, his pulse pounded, and his fangs itched to cut into her flesh. He wanted to feed. He *needed* to feed. On a pretty little demon with a bad attitude. He grabbed the counter behind her to steady himself as a wave of fevered lust ran through him. Lust for her body, or her blood—he didn't know which. He just knew he needed something soon or he was going to snap.

He grinned at her, baring his fangs, and took delight in the little shiver he saw course through her. She could deny it all she wanted, but he saw in her eyes what a turn-on the fangs were for her. *Good.*

He wanted Merida. Any way he could get her. The hunger combined with the beautiful, challenging woman proved to be an intoxicating combination. Sweat broke out across his forehead. His hands clenched into fists so tight he felt his short nails bite into his palms. He hadn't been this out of control in too long to remember. What had been a game turned into something more when she bent over to get something out of a grocery bag on the ground. The last vestiges of his control evaporated into the electrically charged air as his muscles clenched and his mouth watered.

That sweet ass...what he wouldn't give to sink his fangs deep into that firm, round flesh. He licked his lips. He needed...

With a growl of frustration, he slammed his fist into cabinet next to the stove. Merida turned to look at him, her eyes wide with surprise. "What was that for?"

"I haven't eaten in days, I didn't sleep well knowing you were so close, and then you act all high and mighty and like nothing ever happened between us and I want to hurt something. I can't take this. I need..." He let his voice trail off with a low growl.

She straightened, her muscles looking tight, her gaze glancing around the room—ready to bolt, he'd guess by the look on her face. *Sorry, kitty. No running away this time.*

"What do you need?"

He licked his lips as he grinned at her, knowing this was a terrible idea but having no clue how to stop what he'd set it in motion. "Come here, kitty."

"No." She shook her head vigorously, balling her hands into fists. Her glare might tell him to stay away, but her tone lacked conviction.

"*No?*" He smiled at that. He'd have her then, and they both knew it.

"That's what I said. You keep your hands to yourself, Cardoso. I'll kick your ass if you don't."

He'd like to see her try. Really. At this point, maybe some kind of physical confrontation would help him get his mind back where it belonged—on helping Wil with his problem instead of feeding from and fucking a *Panthicenos*. He didn't even know if feeding from her was possible, but at this point, he'd take what he could get.

"You think I'm kidding? I mean it, Cardoso. Back off."

"I don't know if I can."

He reached out for her—and with a sweep of her leg she'd knocked his out from under him. He snagged her wrist as he fell backward. His back smacked the tile floor as Merida landed on top of him in a tangle of limbs. *God.* His cock hardened to the point of pain, her soft flesh pressing against him in a way that only increased his discomfort. She tried to wriggle away, but he rolled her to her back and pinned her down to the floor with his body weight.

He held her down with barely any pressure, securing her wrists to the floor with just one forefinger and thumb. She didn't fight him—not even a token protest. A shiver skittered up his spine when she arched against him. He watched her eyes darken before dropping his gaze to her nipples, puckered under the thin fabric of her t-shirt.

"What the hell do you think you're doing?"

"You're a smart girl. You figure it out." He shifted her under him, moving so that his lower body rested between her thighs. *Much better.* Intense heat ran through him at the contact—her soft, warm skin separated from his by only a little fabric. He remembered the past summer and their too-brief interlude. She'd been so hot, so willing…he needed that feeling again.

"*Royce.*" Her pleading tone nearly destroyed him as her gaze urged him to take what he wanted.

He ran his tongue down the side of her neck, reveling in her sweet-salty skin. He dragged his teeth over her collarbone denying himself—for the moment—all that he needed from her. "When we worked together before, all I thought about was doing this to you. When it happened, it was beyond incredible. And then you walked out on me. It nearly drove me insane."

She snorted. "I don't matter to you. You can have any woman you want. Why bother with bitchy little me?"

He would have laughed at that, if he hadn't been half out of his mind. "You're doing it to me again. Making me crazy. I have to have you." He nipped her earlobe, but made no move to bite in earnest. Not yet. "I can't get enough of you. And this physical stuff gets me hot."

"It does?"

"Oh, yeah." He'd never been fond of strong women until he'd met Merida. He'd always preferred his women to accept what he said without question—until last summer. After her, no one else had satisfied him. He had a sinking suspicion he'd have to search the rest of his life to find another who would. "Tell me something, kitty. Will your blood hurt me?"

He could swear he heard her whimper before she answered. "No. It'll drug you if you drink too much. But unfortunately, it's not going to kill you. For the most part, in human form, I'm human."

"Good."

She gulped, anxiety clouding her expression. What could she be afraid of? "I…uh…why don't I go find you something, anything that—"

"I don't think so. Not when I have a nice, warm body here."

She shook her head vigorously.

"Why not?"

"I can't let you."

He brushed his lips over the side of her neck, trailing his tongue down to her collarbone. "Come on, Merida. Just a little."

"Royce, stop."

The force of her command made him pause. He snapped his gaze up to hers.

"Royce, really. You can't bite me. Trust me, okay? Just stop."

"I don't think I can," he answered just before he sank his fangs deep into the flesh where her shoulder met her neck. Her yelp turned into a moan as he flicked his tongue over the small wound. The flow of her powerful blood gave him a rush, a high feeling. It was the most incredible thing he'd ever experienced. He could easily get addicted to her flavor.

He held her tight against him, his mouth anchoring her in place. He was so turned on he couldn't draw a complete breath. A sexual pull during feeding was normal, but nothing like this. His cock throbbed and threatened to break free of his now too-tight pants. His every nerve tingled and his balls tightened. He broke away well before he'd had enough, but at this rate, he'd embarrass himself by coming in his pants before he got his fill of her.

"My God," he mumbled, panting as much as she was. "I've never felt anything like that in my life."

"Like what?" she breathed.

He rested his lips against her neck and smiled, trying to rein in the impulse to drive into her. If he didn't wait a few minutes and regain some of his control, he'd last all of two thrusts. "Like I could have come right then, just feeding from you."

Shock registered in her gaze, along with a heavy dose of arousal. "You shouldn't have done that."

"I'm sorry. I couldn't help it."

"I tried to warn you. You should have given me a chance to explain. Biting—it sometimes makes me crazy."

"Crazy?" His cock stiffened a little more and he groaned.

"Oh, yeah. *Crazy.*"

She hooked her leg around his and managed to flip him onto his back, her fingers flying to the button and zipper holding his jeans closed. Shocked at her sudden turn, Royce did nothing more than lay back and let her have her way. She was strong, crazed, and he couldn't get enough. His cock throbbed, his balls ached. He needed her. She made him as nuts as he made her, and there was no way in hell he planned on stopping her.

"You're going to hurt yourself," he told her, trying to still the motions of her hands before she scratched herself—or him.

She batted his hands away and yanked at his jeans. He glanced down to see her fingers were now tipped in sharp looking claw-like nails—claws that tore the front of his jeans to shreds. "I'd rather hurt you."

He gulped. "Sounds promising."

She paused, smiling down at him with a wicked gleam in her eyes as she freed his cock from the confines of his boxers and stroked her hand up his length. "It is."

His eyes drifted closed and he lost himself in the moment—at least until she ran those sharp nails down his chest. He winced at the pain, but at the same time, it felt so good. The damned claws were such a huge turn-on. He couldn't help it. He nearly came right then. She ran one thin claw over his erect nipple. It felt amazing. *Jesus.* Instinct and a deep, primal urge to mate took over and he let go. "Get rid of your pants."

She glanced down at his rigid cock once more, her tongue running over her lips, before she pushed off him and stood long enough to strip off her pants. He stood and came up behind her as she started to remove her panties. With a sharp tug to the filmy material, he ripped them from her body. He dropped the ruined fabric to the floor and slid his fingers between her legs. Wet, drenched. He shuddered at the thought of sliding into all that heat.

"Do you know how much I want to fuck you, honey?" he whispered into her ear, finding her clit with his thumb and relishing in the way she wriggled against him. He pressed his front to her back, his cock hard against her soft skin.

"Do it, Royce." She arched back into him, her hands gripping his hips. "*Fuck me.*"

So much for taking it slow and savoring the feel of her near him, surrounding him again. He kicked a chair out away from the table and pushed her toward it, bending her over so that her palms rested on the polished wood surface. He used his knee to spread her legs further apart and slid his fingers into her drenched cunt. She let out a sound somewhere between a moan and a growl. Her inner muscles clamped down on his fingers and a wave of heat washed through his gut. He'd wanted to wait, to tease her a little more to make her pay for the way she'd walked out on him, but that would have to wait. His cock throbbed, needing to be satisfied.

He raised her higher and replaced his fingers with his cock, thrusting into her with enough force to move the chair several inches back until it hit the table. Her body shook and Royce's legs started to weaken. He leaned one hand on the chair back, keeping his other on her hip, as he slammed into her again and again.

He fought the urge to come for as long as he could, but when he felt himself losing the battle he dropped his fingers to the apex of her thighs, stroking his thumb over her clit. It took no more than a few seconds for Merida to come, her body racked with convulsions and her muscles clenching on his cock in a way that drove him over the edge. He groaned as a powerful orgasm ripped through him, destroying him right to the core. He withdrew from her and pulled her up against him, sinking into the chair with her draped over his body.

He nestled his face against her hair, breathing in the scent of warm woman. He'd never felt so sated in his life. But it wouldn't last. He felt her stiffening against him as his breathing settled to a more normal pace. He ticked off seconds in his head, and hadn't even reached five before she'd jumped up and stalked across the room—and out of the kitchen without even a word to him.

"Hey! Where are you going?"

"Shower," she called without looking back.

"Want some company?"

"No." Her heavy footfalls slamming up the stairs echoed her response.

Well. Good thing he didn't care for pillow talk. He'd let her go—this time. One of these days she'd have to stop running. But not tonight. After the way her she'd milked him dry, he didn't think he'd be able to stand up for more than five minutes at a time. He followed her out of the kitchen and up the stairs, but instead of turning right toward the bathroom he made a left and walked into his bedroom.

He stripped out of what was left of his jeans and boxers and flopped down on the bed. He'd never come so hard in his life. One more second and he would have blacked out. That was a scary thought, but exhilarating at the same time. He'd had great sex before. Hell, he'd had phenomenal, mind-blowing, toe-curling sex quite a few times in his long life. But with Merida, it had gone past even that. The last time he'd had her, it had been good. Worthy of a repeat performance. But what had happened in the middle of Wil's kitchen…it had annihilated him. He'd never be the same.

It shook him. *Hard.* Getting her back into bed had started out as a game—a way to prove to her and himself that he wasn't as forgettable as she'd seemed to think. But somehow it had turned into so much more. Somewhere in the middle of her tearing him apart on the floor, he'd come to a realization.

He was hooked.

She had hooked him that first night they'd met. Her attitude intrigued him, her body fascinated him. He wanted more. A lot more. He wanted to spend the next two weeks in her bed, fucking her in every possible position until neither of them could walk. But that wouldn't be possible As much as he appreciated a good loving, he'd never let sex come before work. This would not become the exception.

He sighed and flipped to his back to accommodate his rapidly swelling cock. He hadn't nearly had his fill of her yet. If she thought she could escape by running out of the room, she was dead wrong. Just thinking about her…what she'd done to him…what she'd look like naked and soapy in the shower—*shit*. Whether or not she wanted company, she'd get it.

He stomped into the bathroom and threw back the shower curtain. Merida gasped, her eyes widening as her lips parted. Flushed pink and shiny from her washing, she looked good enough to eat. He smiled at the thought. Pulling her from the shower, he lifted her into his arms and settled her ass on the edge of the vanity, spreading her legs with his hands.

"What do you think you're doing? I'm soaked. I need to dry off."

He shook his head. "Don't even think about it. I prefer you wet, kitty."

He didn't give her time to respond before he dove in, plunging his tongue deep into her cunt. One of her hands flew to his hair, grasping large handfuls and tugging in a way that crossed the line between pleasure and pain. He loved the way her hands felt on his head, her fingers curling against his scalp as she moaned softly. He couldn't get enough.

And the way she tasted—just a lap and he felt like he'd go out of his mind. There was definitely something about this whole demon thing. Would a human woman ever satisfy him again? He seriously doubted it. He sucked her clit into his mouth, using his lips and teeth to bring her to the edge. Her moans grew louder, her fingers tightening in his hair, and she shuddered in orgasm. He swirled his tongue over her clit until her spasms subsided before standing and pulling her into his arms. She didn't fight him this time. She wrapped her arms around his neck and buried her face against his bare chest instead, as if she'd known how much he needed it.

That thought stopped him in his tracks. Where the hell did that come from? He didn't need her. He didn't need anyone. He didn't do relationships, couldn't handle commitment. He was just in it for the sex. Every time.

Yeah, right, spoke a little voice in the back of his head. *Not this time.*

He mentally told the voice shut up. He didn't have time to get involved. He only had time to get her into bed. That was *all* he wanted to do.

The little nagging voice got a little louder. *Yeah, and that's why you dragged her all the way up here when Eric would have done just fine. Because of work.*

Because he knew how close to the truth the voice was, and because he didn't like it at all, he did the only thing he could think of to banish it from his head. He stood up and thrust his cock into her cunt, still contracting from her orgasm. Her head flung back, her hair dripping water into the sink, tiny goose bumps peppering her naked skin. God, he loved her skin. It was so soft, so warmly tanned—silky and smooth. He wanted nothing more than to lie over her, his skin covering hers, to feel her curves pressed against him he stroked into her slowly, tenderly—

Fuck. Why was his mind stuck on this whole *tender*

thing?

"God, Royce," Merida moaned. He looked down at her, but he couldn't hold eye contact. That would do him in. Instead, he focused his gaze on her lips—full and naturally dark pink. So sexy. So *goddamned* sexy. He wanted to feel them, hot and moist, wrapped around his cock. Oh, yeah. He liked this train of thought much better. Now he had his mind back where he wanted it—on the act itself and not the emotions better left alone.

He thrust harder, the feel of her nails digging into his shoulders blurring his vision. He leaned down and took one of her peaked nipples between his teeth, rolling the erect flesh gently. When he had her gasping for breath, he moved on to the other nipple, laving it with long, slow, swirling strokes. When he pulled back, he made the mistake of looking into her eyes. The emotions he saw there mirrored what he felt inside, rough and raw and deep. Her questioning gaze snagged his, tugged at his heart. She wasn't nearly as cold as she wanted everyone to think. Not even close. The realization nearly broke him. "Merida, I—"

She silenced him with a finger on his lips. "Don't think right now, okay?"

He couldn't agree more. Thinking, in this particular situation, had become very dangerous to his mental health. He tried to push his concentration to the purely physical. He gripped her hips and thrust harder into her just as her body tightened and she shuddered with another climax. He followed her soon after, biting into her shoulder as his release slammed through him. She dug her heels into his ass and held him there, milking his cock completely. He glanced down at her, at the same questioning, confused look in her eyes. Not knowing what else to do, he leaned down and kissed her.

Uncertainty ate at his senses, every cell in his body screaming that she was the one. But she couldn't be. He'd met the one woman right for him—and lost her four hundred years ago. He wasn't willing to risk his heart again. He broke the kiss and, with a heavy sigh, picked Merida up and carried her to his bed. He planned to keep her there for the rest of the night—if not longer.

Chapter Seven

Royce rolled over in the big bed, the sense of a warm body next to him filling his subconscious. He sighed and wrapped his arms around the woman next to him. Merida. The one woman he hadn't been able to get his mind off during the past year. Every other woman—and there hadn't been as many as she'd seemed to think—had *been* her. He worried about her reaction to what they'd done. Would she run away like she had before? He hoped she wouldn't. He didn't want to be responsible for driving her away when Wil needed her help.

Her tongue ran down the length of his arm and he tangled his fingers in her warm soft…*fur*?

He jumped out of bed, his feet smacking the cold hardwood floor as his gaze hit the giant cat in bed with him. He backed into the wall and blinked at the animal. "What the fuck do you think you're doing, Merida?"

She jumped off the bed with feline grace, stalking toward him on huge black paws. She stopped in front of him and rubbed her head against his leg, her tail wrapping around his bare calf. He stood in front of her, bare naked, and didn't like the way her glowing green eyes focused on certain parts.

"Stop it. That's enough."

He could swear he saw her smile. Her cat form shifted and morphed, turning into the human he liked much better. His breathing slowed as she stood, dragging her palms up his body. "What's the matter, stud? Can't handle a little kitty cat first thing in the morning?"

Was it morning already? Shit. How had he managed to sleep through an entire night? A quick glance at the clock confirmed what she said. It was a little after six in the morning. He moved away from her and dug out some clothes. "Get dressed, *kitty*. We've got a few things to discuss before I go to bed."

"How can you possibly be tired? You slept most of the night."

"Yeah, and you damn near killed me yesterday evening. I'm not exactly young. I need some time to recover."

And some time to get over the shock of going to bed with a woman and waking up with a cat. He let out a harsh breath. Things didn't seem as perfect in the light of day as they had the night before.

* * * * *

"You knew what I was when you slept with me, idiot. If you can't handle it, stay out of my bed." She should have known something like this would happen. Yes, she'd deliberately provoked him, waking him up in cat form, but she'd had to know. She'd seen something in his eyes the night before that had led her to believe…something she had no business hoping for. She knew Royce well enough to understand his aversion to commitment.

She grabbed the sheet off the bed and wrapped it around her. "What were you thinking, anyway? Why did you even touch me?"

"Gee, I don't know. Maybe that we should take advantage of the mutual chemistry between us?"

She snorted. "Damn it, if you hadn't—"

"Oh, don't you start that now. You're not going to go blaming this on me. You're the one who…"

She watched him struggle for a response until he finally gave in and shook his head. "Okay, fine. Maybe this time it was my fault. But I didn't hear you trying to stop me. *Not once.* You wanted what happened just as much as I did. You told me to fuck you!"

Her face flamed and she had to turn away to prevent him from seeing how he affected her. The hum of her blood, the increase in her heartbeat, the moisture that pooled between her legs—whenever he got close, her body reacted that way. "Okay. Fine. I practically begged you to fuck me. I wanted you. At the time. But now that I can think clearly, I realize what a mistake it was. Again. I don't want anything to do with you."

"Bullshit."

Bullshit? Yeah. It was. She swiped a hand across her forehead. "I'm sorry. We were both stressed. You offered comfort. I took it."

"*Comfort?* Woman, are you out of your mind? There wasn't anything remotely *comforting* about what happened. It was sex—in its most basic and elemental state. And it was amazing. Better than last time. Better than anything." He stepped closer and drew his finger down the center of her throat to the hollow of her collarbone, flicking gently. "Do you have a problem with dirty, kitty?"

His voice held a husky promise that brought to mind the tearing of clothing, hot and sweaty bodies, illicit uncontrolled sex—she ducked away and moved across the room. Just his scent alone was enough to soak her panties if she'd been wearing any. And the way he called her kitty—it should have pissed her off. It should have made her want to rip his head off. It didn't. It made her want to rip his *clothes* off instead.

"Do you have a problem with dirty?" he asked again, coming up behind her. His breath tickled her shoulder as he spoke. "Answer my question."

"No, I don't have a problem with dirty." She spun on him, her hands on her hips. "I have a problem with *vampires*. I can't stand them. *Panthicenos* and vampires don't get along. It's a fact of life."

He leaned back against the wall, his arms crossed over his chest, a self-satisfied grin plastered on his chiseled face. "Seems to me we got along fine up until a few minutes ago."

For crying out loud! She growled in frustration. What had she ever done in her life to deserve this kind of torture? "If we get along so well, bloodsucker, why is it that I want to tear you apart right now?"

He leaned closer and nipped her earlobe. "Sounds like a plan to me."

Okay. That's it. "This is getting us nowhere. I have to go find Wil."

She nearly smiled at the jealous irritation that flashed in his eyes when she mentioned Wil's name. "Why do you need to find him?"

"He said he'd try to get me the information I need. Remember? I'm going to get dressed and go downstairs to wait. I would think he'll be here soon if he's not already."

She swung the door open and jumped back in surprise when she saw Wil standing there, his hand poised to knock. She tightened her grip on the sheet as his gaze moved down her body. "Do you mind?"

He shrugged with an indifference that bothered her. "Sorry. You flash it in my face, of course I'm gonna look. I'm a guy. Anyway, I called a friend at the library and got her to dig up some information for you. I wanted to drop it by before I head into town for a…uh, meeting. I heard yelling. I wanted to make sure you two weren't killing each other."

"Well, I guess you came at the right time, because I was just about to strangle your friend. He'll have to thank you for saving his life."

She pushed past Wil and hurried down the hall to her room. Once safely behind the closed door, she flopped against it and slid to the floor. What had she gotten herself into?

Chapter Eight

Michelle faced Wil over her coffee cup, her eyes narrowed. She tapped her fingernails against the cup handle, the noise grating on his already frayed nerves. "Something very strange is going on here."

"I'm inclined to agree with you there." *And you don't even know the half of it.*

"So are you going to tell me what it is?"

He raised an eyebrow at the question he'd been expecting since arriving ten minutes earlier. "What makes you think I have any idea what you're talking about?"

She let out a sigh as her gaze dropped to the table. A familiar-looking waitress stopped by the table and set down Michelle's plate of breakfast. Her uncertain gaze flickered to Wil. "Are you sure I can't get you anything?"

"No, thanks. Just the water is fine."

She gave a small shrug as she turned to walk away. "Suit yourself."

Michelle cleared her throat. "You're acting a little odd this morning, William." She reached across the table and brushed her fingers against the back of Wil's hand. He pulled back.

"Am I?" He took a sip of his water, swirling the straw around in the glass and clinking the ice cubes together. "I hadn't noticed."

He stifled a yawn, wanting only to be back at home in bed. Hopefully she'd get to her point quickly and he could leave. He didn't want to be anywhere near her, but he didn't want to miss any information she had that might help Merida.

"Yes. Do you think it's normal to wear sunglasses in a restaurant? It's not even that bright in here."

"It's bright enough." He pushed the sunglasses further up his nose and leaned back against the worn vinyl-covered bench. "I worked last night. I'm tired, and my eyes are sensitive."

She shook her head, her expression telling him she clearly didn't believe him, but she let it go. "Something about those murders has you worried. I'd like to know what it is."

He heaved a sigh and ran his hands down his face. Damn it. He'd be lucky if he didn't fall asleep behind the wheel on the way home. "Nothing special. The whole situation is troubling. Any murder, especially here, tends to cause a bit of worry."

"But this is different." She pinned him with an accusing glare. "Isn't it?"

"Well, it isn't every day that people are mutilated in Caswell. Did you invite me here to interview me? Cause I've got to tell you, after a long night I'm not really in the mood."

"No. I didn't." Her tongue darted out to wet her lips and hunger curled low in his gut. "I'm worried. Things have been a little...odd lately."

He sat up, his interest now piqued by her halting sentence—and her anxious tone of voice. "What do you mean?"

"You're going to think this sounds kooky, but I've been having these weird dreams." She tucked a stray curl behind her ear and tried to smile. Her attempt fell flat, her face paling a shade. "I've been dreaming about my father. Did I ever tell you about him?"

Wil shook his head. He had a feeling he wouldn't like where this was going. "I don't think you have."

"He'd never wanted kids. At least that's what my mother told me growing up. That was why he'd never wanted to see me." She gave a shaky laugh before her expression once again grew serious. "He was a real estate developer in Texas. He cared more about his work than raising a family, so he divorced my mother when she got pregnant with me. She moved to Caswell to live with her sister after my father kicked her out."

She paused and sighed, pushing her untouched food around her plate with her fork. When she looked up at him again, he saw the pain clearly in her gaze—along with a good dose of fear. He waited on edge to hear the rest of her story. This could be the break they'd been looking for.

"Is your father still alive?" he asked when she remained silent.

She shook her head. "He was killed when I was ten. My mother told me he'd had a heart attack, but once I was old enough to be curious about her story, I did some research and found out he'd been murdered."

Wil leaned forward, hanging on her every word. Something Merida had said came back to him. *Either the demon is attached to the property, or to a person.* Had the truth about the murders been right in front of him the whole time? "Did they ever catch the murderer?"

"No. I asked my mom about it, but she refused to talk." She closed her eyes, looking close to tears. "She killed herself not too long after I tried to talk to her about it, so I never got the chance to ask again."

He'd known Michelle's mother had committed suicide a few years ago, but he didn't know the details. "How did she die?"

Michelle blinked up at him, anger and confusion in her eyes. "What?"

"How did she die?" he repeated, his heart racing. "How exactly did she take her life?"

"She slit her wrists. God, Wil, do you have to be so morbid?"

"Occupational hazard." No one had ever accused him of having too much tact. "Sorry if I upset you."

Her glare softened a little and she shrugged. "Whatever. I know you don't care about anything involving emotions, but it hurt when my mom killed herself. I know I hadn't been the best daughter, but I'd tried. I just couldn't be what she expected me to be."

"And what was that?"

"Good. I couldn't seem to stay out of trouble."

Ideas began clicking in his head, too fast for him to latch onto anything specific. He didn't know much about demons and their capabilities, but Michelle's story sounded a little strange. He made a show of checking the time on his watch. "You know what? I have to get home and get some sleep. It's going to be another long night, and I don't want to be tired." He needed to get back and discuss the latest twist with Merida. He took out his wallet and handed Michelle a twenty. "This should take care of your meal, and the tip. I'll give you a call later, okay?"

He was already out the door and halfway to the side street where he'd parked his car when she caught up with him. "Where are you running off to? I asked you to meet me so we could have a talk. I didn't expect you to run out fifteen minutes after you got here."

"I'm leaving. You know how it is. I've got to get some sleep before I drop." Sleep was now the furthest thing from his mind.

She glared at him with a mix of irritation and anxiety that caused him to draw up short. "I would have thought you, of all people, would be willing to listen to my story."

"I did listen, didn't I?"

"Only part of it. I didn't get to tell you about my dreams."

He sighed in resignation as he leaned his hip on one of the green painted benches that lined the sidewalk. "Okay. Tell me about them."

She shook her head, her breath coming in shallow gasps. "It doesn't matter. You don't care."

"Obviously it mattered, or you wouldn't have asked me to meet you." He tried to focus on Michelle, but the sun beating on his skin killed him. He felt like he was being eaten alive. After having no sleep the night before, his resistance had gotten too low to spend any lengthy amount of time outside during the day. He didn't want to end up with permanent scarring.

"The dreams… I don't remember much about them. They're an odd, jumbled mess that I can barely recall when I wake up. But they remind me of something my mother always told me growing up."

"What is that?"

"That my father had sold his soul to the devil, and that was why I couldn't control myself."

A cold chill shot through Wil and he sucked in a sharp

breath. The devil? Not possible. But a demon…he needed to discuss this with Merida. Maybe Michelle had simply been a high-strung child. Or maybe she had deeper, far more sinister problems.

"I know she didn't mean it," Michelle said softly. "Not really. But, well, I don't know what to think. I guess I just thought you should know about that. I don't know how, but it might help with your investigation."

He pushed away from the bench and walked toward his car, the noise of the birds chirping combined with everything running through his head giving him a headache. "Thanks. I'm sure it's nothing, but I appreciate the thought."

She ran after him, snagging the back of his shirt with her fingers. "Stop running away! I'm trying to tell you something here. Why can't you be there for me when I need you?"

"I know what happened to your neighbors hit you hard, but I can't discuss any of that with you. You know that. With your job, you should be a little more understanding."

"Why should I give you understanding when you can't give it to me?" There was a pleading look in her eyes he couldn't decipher — and didn't care to.

He had more important things to think about than an attention-starved reporter looking for a good story. And if half of what she'd told him today was true, he had to get back to Merida right away with the information before someone else got hurt. If the demon had been attached to Michelle's father, or family, anyone around her could be in a lot of danger.

"We'll talk about it later. Why don't I take you out in a

couple of days?"

She shook her head, a flash of panic lighting her eyes for a brief moment before anger replaced it. "I don't think so. You were right to try to break this off a couple weeks ago. A cup of coffee before we go back to my place and spend a few hours in bed doesn't exactly constitute a date. You don't even spend the night, and you refuse to see me anytime during the day. It's more like you want me around when you want to screw, but completely ignore me when you're not in the mood."

He should have known better than to get involved with a human. It always ended in trouble. "I'm glad you finally see things my way. If you want to talk, call me tomorrow when you've had a chance to cool off."

She pushed past him on the way to her car, which she'd parked in front of his. "I'm not the one who needs to cool off, Wil. You need to get your priorities straight."

"I have them straight. First is solving those murders. Everything else has to wait."

"I could help you with them, if you'd stop being such a jerk long enough to listen."

He stopped as he opened his car door and turned back to her. What more could she do for him than the information she'd already given—*if* it turned out to be valid. "What do you think you can do for me that I can't do for myself?"

She opened her mouth to speak, but he stopped her. "No, really. Think about this. Tell me one thing you can do for me that I'm not perfectly capable of doing. One thing that doesn't involve sex."

"It's that woman, isn't it?"

"What woman?"

"The one staying in your house. You're sleeping with her, aren't you?"

Of all the nerve… "No, I'm not sleeping with Merida. Why are you suddenly obsessed with my sex life?"

"Because I thought I was your sex life."

He let out a long, slow breath. He didn't know what to believe anymore. Part of him didn't want to hurt her, but a larger, louder part wanted to show her the fling had ended. He couldn't continue on with a woman he didn't trust, and all the talk about demons and deals with the devil might just be another way to get her hooks into him all over again. "Did you really think this thing between us was exclusive?"

She shook her head as she yanked open her car door. "Fine. If that's what you want, you've got it. Have a nice life, Wil." She got into her car, slammed the door, and peeled away from the curb. As he watched her take the corner onto Main Street, he said a silent prayer that she wouldn't get into an accident. He didn't need her to get herself killed. He already had enough on his mind this morning.

He got into his own car and followed her through the streets, stopping a few hundred feet from her house as she pulled up in front of it. He watched her get out of her car and walk through her front door, her shoulders hunched and her face red—probably from crying. He should feel bad for the way he'd treated her, but he couldn't bring himself to care about her anymore. She'd ruined that with her unpredictable behavior and the way she'd used him. He didn't mind being used, but only on his terms—and not for information.

Chapter Nine

Merida sat on her bedroom floor with her legs folded up under her. She breathed deeply, blocking out the world around her, her mind focused on one thing. The psychic ropes. She felt closer this time than she had any other time. She knew deep inside that this would be it. Today would be the day she finally got it right. After all this—

"What's going on?"

She snapped her eyes open to find Royce standing in the doorway, shielding his eyes from the sun streaming through the open windows. She narrowed her eyes at him. "What the hell are you doing out of bed? It's only seven-thirty."

"Couldn't sleep." He gave her a half smile she would have found sexy if she hadn't been so irritated. "I keep thinking about last night, about you and me."

Who was she kidding? She found everything about the man sexy, despite her current aggravation. She flopped back on the floor and closed her eyes. "Jerk."

"What did I do?"

She opened one eye long enough to see that he'd moved further into the room. He walked past her to the windows and started pulling the drapes closed. Men. *Vampires.* "I'm kinda busy here. Do you think you can stop that and leave?"

He shrugged, and she wanted to smack the humorous look off his face. He was *so* not funny sometimes. The mattress springs groaned as he sat down. "What do you think of this whole mess?"

Wasn't it usually the woman who analyzed things to death the next day? "What happened, happened. We can't take it back, we can't change it, but—"

His burst of laughter cut short her train of thought. She opened both eyes and glared at him. "What's so funny?"

"I'm talking about the murders."

"Oh."

"Yeah. *Oh.* So tell me, kitty, what's your gut reaction to this situation?"

She sighed heavily and raised her fingers in the air, letting a blue spark fly toward the ceiling. "I can't do anything about it until later, so I'm trying not to think about it at all."

"What's your general impression? I'm not trying to pressure you into action when it isn't the time for it; I just want to hear your feelings on the situation. Do you think it's related to the property?"

She shook her head and pushed herself into a sitting position. "I looked over the paperwork Wil brought me on the house. Nothing. No shady past at all. The trees were cleared fifty years ago, the duplex built thirty years ago, and nothing strange, at least nothing recorded, has ever happened there. So I guess we'll have to go with the second option."

"The demon is connected to a person."

"Yeah." She stood and walked to the windows, opening the curtains to let in the warm spring breeze. "How well do you know Wil?"

"I've known him for most of my life."

She didn't dare turn back to look at him as she issued her next question. "Is he capable of violence?"

Royce hesitated a little too long before he answered, and when he spoke, his tone sounded strained. "Why do you ask?"

"Because I think he's somehow connected to this whole mess."

"Bullshit. Don't you think he would have noticed?" He came up behind her and put his hands on her shoulders, spinning her roughly around. "Where do you get off saying things like that about a man who's been nothing but nice to you?"

"It's just a feeling I get, okay?" She ducked out from under his hard stare and paced the length of the room. "I think we can sometimes be blind to the truth, ignoring what we don't want to be there when it upsets us."

"Are you trying to say you think I'm blind to what's really going on?"

"I'm not sure." She stopped in front of him and crossed her arms over her chest, refusing to be intimidated by an overgrown bloodsucker with a temper. "Maybe he doesn't even know. I don't know what to tell you. You asked me here to help—either take it or leave it."

Royce shook his head. "I still don't see why you think Wil is connected to all this."

"I don't know. He isn't in contact with the demon—I would have seen that when I first met him. But he knows something, even if he refuses to see it yet."

"Are you going to tell him what you think?"

A tricky question, one she hadn't spent much time

thinking about. If she talked to him about it, maybe he could give her a decent lead. Then again, maybe it would cause him to do something stupid in his search for the killer. She couldn't risk it. "I don't want him to know. Not yet. We'll have an easier chance to draw the person out if he doesn't go snooping around. Besides, I don't think he'd believe me, anyway."

Royce tilted his head to the side as he looked down at her. "Why not?"

"He's just like you. Typical stubborn male. Always wanting to get his way."

"That's a little harsh, don't you think? You don't even know the guy. What is it you have against men?"

"Nothing." Just a thousand years worth of being coddled, of being treated like a second-rate citizen because she happened to be born female. Being told what to do, because they "thought it was best for her". She couldn't tell him any of that. He'd never understand. Frustrated, she let a jolt of electricity slip off her fingers and she watched it spiral up into the air before it disappeared with a poof.

Royce's eyes widened. "What are you doing?"

She snorted. "Blowing off some steam." She let another jolt go, and then another, before she decided to play with something stronger. The worried look on his face coupled with the way he backed up a few steps made her smile. She loved to see a big, strong man want to run and hide when she got going.

She wiggled her fingers in the air until they were tipped with fire. She raised them in Royce's direction, the flames licking in the air with burning intensity. When he showed no signs of backing away further, she fisted her hands and the flames disappeared with a snap. "I've been trying something new, but it's just not working."

"Anything I can help with?"

His answer surprised her. She smiled, entertaining the fleeting thought of Royce bound to the bed with the ropes, helpless to her exploring hands. And tongue. She liked that idea. A lot. In theory. The ropes wouldn't last long enough for that kind of activity, but she could always dream. "Maybe."

He braced his hands behind him on the windowsill. The movement caused his chest and arm muscles to bulge in a way she found fascinating. She could use a little distraction at the moment, and a nice-looking guy like Royce could provide plenty of that. For hours on end, as evidenced by the night before. She smiled and licked her lips as her eyes landed on the front placket of his jeans— and the erection that already bulged against them. "Impressive, vampire."

He laughed, somewhat nervously. "What can I say? I've been like this since you walked out on me earlier."

"Am I making you nervous?"

"Of course not." He tried to look casual, but she saw the truth in his eyes. What she was scared him. He didn't like it, and he probably didn't like the chemistry between them. Her smile widened and her palms started to tingle like crazy.

She lifted her hands to her face and saw what she'd been waiting a year to see. Thin, pale blue ropes arced from her fingers, stretching out into the air in front of her. They disappeared when she wiggled her fingers, but she knew now that she could call them whenever she wanted them. She laughed as exhilaration filled her. "I did it!"

A wicked idea formed in her head and she smiled at him. "Watch this, vampire."

With a twist of her finger in the air, she pretended to stretch a rope around his neck. And then it was there—her very own psychic rope collar, complete with leash. She gave it a tug and he stumbled forward. "Man, I'm good."

Royce glared at her as his fingers tried to pry the rope of his neck. "What the hell are you doing?"

She gave the rope another tug, pulling him closer to her. He tried to dig in his heels, but couldn't manage. She imagined the choking sensation he got when he tried to hold still had something to do with the nasty look in his eyes. She loved every second of it. "What's the matter, tough guy? Afraid of being tied up?" One more tug and he stood right in front of her. She ran a hand up his chest, her fingernail dragging across his flat nipple. And then the worst thing that could possibly happen happened.

The ropes flickered and dissolved into the air.

Royce's answering smile was nothing short of predatory and a shiver ran through her. "I'm not afraid. Are *you*?"

Uh-oh. The heated, dominating look in his eyes made her want to turn and run out of the room. It also dampened her panties and made her legs weak. She opened her mouth to speak, but no sound came out. She shook her head.

He leaned in and ran his tongue down the side of her neck, leaving a trail of quivering skin in his wake. She frowned. Since when did she *quiver*?

"Trust me, kitty?" he asked, his breath hot and moist against her ear.

She gulped as he scraped his fangs over her earlobe.

"Um, I think so."

"You started this game with your little rope trick. Keep that in mind." He pushed her back until her legs hit the bed. "I believe it's my turn to play now."

Her stomach flip-flopped at his sudden change in attitude. She'd never seen him like this before. She shouldn't like it, but she did. "And what do you have in mind?"

He didn't say anything, but he really didn't have to. If she went by the look on his face, she was now in some very deep trouble. She swallowed hard against the lust raging inside her. This kind of behavior shouldn't turn her on. She needed to say something, do something to put him in his place. She opened her mouth, but when he reached into her suitcase and pulled out a pair of thigh-high stockings, she clamped it shut again.

"Why haven't you worn these for me?" he asked, his heated gaze boring straight into hers.

Her voice sounded rough, husky when she answered. "I brought them to go with my dress, in case I needed to wear something fancier than jeans and a t-shirt. I like to be prepared for anything. I never know what a job is going to bring."

He let out a breath and shook his head, his voice quiet yet commanding at the same time. "I thought you brought them for me."

"What use would you have for them?" As soon as the words left her mouth, she wanted to bite them back. She knew exactly what use he had for them, and she refused to give him that kind of control. No man deserved that much trust. "Royce?"

His smile displayed the fangs that made her stomach

flutter and her panties drench. If she gave in to him, she'd be lost. He'd want it this way again, with her at his total mercy, and the idea made her flinch. It did other things to her, also, things she refused to acknowledge. She wouldn't let herself be thought of as weak. If her traitorous body would listen to reason, she might be able to tell him to stop.

"How much do you want me?" he asked.

She closed her eyes, not sure how to answer his question. If she told him the truth, he'd know he had her right where he wanted her. If she lied and told him she wasn't interested, he'd probably walk away and leave her so aroused she couldn't think straight.

"It's just for fun." He lifted her chin with his finger and looked down at her. The sincerity she saw in his eyes nearly undid her. "Nothing serious. I promise. It can be very pleasurable to *play* sometimes, if you'll trust me."

She melted at the way he said *play*. Her heart thudded in her chest, her blood roared in her ears. The demanding expression on his face sent her over the edge, out of the realm of comfort and into new territory, where she had to relinquish all control to Royce in order to receive the pleasure his gaze promised. "Okay. Do whatever you want."

"Anything?"

She shrugged, trying *not* to look nervous as hell and way out of her element. "Sure. Why not."

From his knowing smile, she knew he didn't buy a second of her bravado. He moved away from the bed his arms crossed over his chest, her thigh-highs hanging from one hand. "Strip."

She tried not to melt into a puddle on the floor.

"Excuse me?" Her voice faltered, as well as her legs, and she stumbled to the side. Why had she never known how much of a turn-on this could be?

He raised an eyebrow in impatience. "You heard me. Take off your clothes and get on the bed."

Not knowing what to do, she stood there, her legs against the bed and her hands on her hips.

He took a step closer, crowding her with his size and his presence. "Scared, kitty?"

"Of course not." Scared? Not exactly. More like so turned on she could barely stand up. But if he thought she was going to make this easy for him, he'd better think again. "Why don't you strip first?"

He let out a harsh breath, his predatory smile turning into a frown. "Well, if you don't want to play by the rules, we don't have to play at all." He pivoted on his heel and started to walk toward the door.

What? No. He couldn't do that to her. She needed him. *Desperately.* She refused to let him walk away. "Hold on. Fine. I'll strip."

He turned slowly, regarding her with a curious gaze. A corner of his mouth rose in a half-smile as she pulled off her shirt and unbuttoned her jeans. She shucked the jeans, along with her panties and socks, and pulled off her bra. The whole process couldn't have taken more than a few minutes, but with Royce's gaze glued to her body, scrutinizing every move, it felt like an eternity.

"Happy now?" she asked when she stood before him, nude and shivering from the heat in his eyes.

He smiled, but shook his head. "Not yet. Get on the bed."

She sat back on the firm mattress, the satiny material

of the comforter rubbing against her wet pussy in a very desirable way. Not knowing what to do with her arms, she dropped them to her side. "What now?"

"Lay down on your back." He ran his tongue over his fangs and she gulped.

She scooted back on the mattress, her legs no stronger than gelatin, and let herself flop back. He moved closer to the side of the bed and stood staring down at her, his intensity setting her nerves on edge and arousing her beyond belief. Her whole body shook with anticipation— and a good amount of fear.

"Reach up and grab the headboard," he told her. She blew out a breath as she did as told, grasping the slats of the headboard in her hands. She looked up as he looped one stocking through the headboard and tied one end around each of her wrists, tethering her to the bed. She could move her arms, but not much. She wouldn't be going anywhere anytime soon. He trailed his big, hot hands down her arms, along the sides of her breasts, to her waist. His fingers dug into her sides and he stared down at her, seeming to search her face for something.

"Do you know how long I've been waiting to get you into this position?"

Not trusting her voice, she shook her head.

He moved a hand to her stomach, splaying his fingers. They stretched nearly from hip to hip. "Too long. Too damned long," he mumbled, his gaze now fixed on her stomach.

"Are you going to undress?"

He didn't look at her when he answered. "Not yet." Instead, he did something that had her gasping for breath. He flipped her onto her stomach.

Anxiety rose in her, sharp and strong. "What are you doing?"

She got her answer when she felt something soft brush across her legs. She flinched. "What's that?"

He held the other stocking up in the air, waving it like a victory flag. "Would you rather I used something with a little more substance?"

"No," she nearly yelled. He probably meant something leather. *How could this possibly turn her on?* So much for being a modern woman in control of her body and her choices. In a few short minutes, Royce had broken apart everything she thought she knew about herself and twisted her inside out.

He must have felt her unease, because he nudged her legs apart and ran the tips of his fingers over her pussy. "So wet. I need to taste you." She felt his hot breath against her sensitive skin just before his tongue ran the length of her slit, from anus to clit. Already beyond aroused, she cried out as his tongue swirled over her clit. She arched her back, thrusting her pussy closer to his mouth, but he pushed her back down to the mattress and pulled his mouth away. "Relax. I can't have you coming too quickly."

She whimpered. "Why not?"

"You're asking entirely too many questions. No more. Keep your mouth shut and enjoy."

He spread her legs further apart, pushing his fingers between her thighs. He dipped a finger into her cunt, stroking in and out a few times before withdrawing. And then she felt the soft slap of his hand against her ass. She stiffened. "What the hell do you think you're doing?"

"No talking, remember?"

"But—"

She snapped her mouth shut as his hand descended on her ass again, three times, each spanking a little harder than the last. She shifted, her pussy growing wetter by the second.

"Royce." She mentally chastised herself when his name came out as no more than a moan. She wasn't supposed to get turned on from spanking. Strong women didn't let men take control, didn't let them do things like *this*. Yet, she couldn't remember ever being this wet. She felt like she could come just from the light sting of his palm against her skin. "I'm not into play this rough."

He laughed, his fingers dipping into her cunt and his thumb circling her clit. "Your body says otherwise." Intense pressure built inside her, but just as she felt the first stirrings of orgasm, he pulled back again.

He brought his palm down on her three more times, leaving tingling skin as he lifted his hand away. She moaned and writhed against the bed, wishing she had her hands free so she could make herself come. He didn't seem to be in any rush, and she might explode if she waited too much longer. All those times she'd wondered what women saw in this kind of sex…now she knew the truth. Thinking about being tied up and spanked, and actually being in the situation were two very different things. She loved every second.

This time when he spanked her, he thrust his fingers inside her at the same time. Hard. His thumb circled her clit again and she bit her lip to hold back a cry. It felt so amazing. She couldn't hold it back much longer, yet he'd told her he didn't want her to come. When he pressed his thumb down on her clit, he whispered, "Come for me, kitty."

Her orgasm took her with such force it knocked the

breath from her lungs. She struggled to breathe, struggled to stay conscious as spasms seized her body. When he finally backed away, she felt like she was floating on a cloud, somewhere where nothing mattered but how she felt and what he could do to her. She never wanted to come down.

His hand massaging her ass brought her back to reality and she shuddered at the touch. She glanced over her shoulder and found him looking down at her with something that looked a lot like tenderness. Her heart pounded as he smiled. "You're beautiful," he murmured as he stood and stripped off his jeans and boxers.

His words shook her more than they had the right to. Why would he be so nice to her? This was only about sex, right? Somewhere along the way, the line between sex and something more had blurred. He stood over her, looking nervous and unsure and very aroused. The urge to pull him close, front to front, overwhelmed her. "Untie me."

He started to shake his head, but she cut him off.

"Please, Royce. Untie me. I want to be able to hold you when you're inside me."

When he made no move to free her, she stretched her hands out and wrapped her fingers around the stocking, melting away the nylon straps with a flash of fire.

He barked a strained laugh. "You could have gotten out the whole time?"

She nodded.

"So why didn't you?"

"I can't explain it." She rolled to her back and reached her arms out to him. "I didn't want to."

He joined her on the bed, fitting himself between her parted thighs. His cock slid along her pussy and she arched against him. She wrapped her arms around his neck and pulled him down for a kiss, the rush of emotions she felt scaring her. When had she started to care about him so much? It unnerved her to think that he might mean something to her beyond a quick fling or a business partner of sorts. She tried to tell herself she couldn't let it happen, but she had a feeling she was too late. The fall had already begun, and it would be only a matter of time before... She shook her head, not willing to think such thoughts. Not yet. Not so soon. She broke the kiss to trail her lips across his jaw and down the side of his neck, delighting in the shiver she wrung from him.

"Is there anything that will hold you?" he asked, his voice hoarse.

She hesitated before she answered. "Well, there are special cuffs and chains I've heard are made for those with more...power, but I think they're really expensive."

"It would be worth it."

He meant more to her than she cared to admit. For now, she'd be content with holding him, letting him know through her actions that she needed him.

God. She *needed* him. She'd never needed anyone in her life, except for maybe Eric and Sam. But *never* anyone in this capacity. What was she going to do? She'd tried so hard to avoid anything that might complicate the job at hand, but she hadn't banked on *this*.

That was *all*. She didn't need to fall in love. Because with Royce, that *wouldn't* happen.

"Are you okay?" he asked softly, gazing down at her with worry in his eyes. "You seem far away."

"Yeah. You didn't hurt me, if that's what you mean."

"Good. Did you enjoy yourself?"

"Yes." The escaped before she could stop it. She rushed to cover it up. "But don't get any ideas. Don't think that's going to happen every time."

"Every time? There will be more times than this morning?" His lips curved into a slow smile. "I thought you didn't even like me."

"I don't have to like you personally to like sex with you. We don't have to get along to fu —"

He leaned in and kissed her softly on the lips, stopping the rest of her sentence. "Would it really be that bad to like me?"

She snorted noncommittally.

"Come on, Merida. Admit it. You like me." To punctuate his request, he eased his cock into her soaked cunt and stroked in and out with maddening slowness.

Her breath caught. "Yeah, okay. Maybe I do. But just a little. Don't go getting an inflated ego over it."

"Wouldn't dream of it." He nuzzled his face against her throat. Just the touch of his lips against her skin made her shiver. "We don't have to put boundaries on what we have. We both know we're not going to get along a hundred percent of the time. We also know we're good together, and I'm not talking about just the sex. Why don't we just see where this takes us, and not put on any limitations?"

"Okay."

His strokes quickened, his breathing growing more labored. "You feel so incredible around me. I don't think I can hold back much longer."

"So don't." She wrapped her legs around his waist and dug in with her heels, pulling him tighter against her. Four thrusts later, she felt his body tighten as he came with a long, drawn-out moan. When he collapsed on top of her, she stroked his back and kissed his shoulder.

After a few minutes, Royce rolled over, tucking her against his side and pulling the sheet over them. His eyes were closed when she glanced up, his mouth set in a satisfied smile. "How are you doing?"

His eyelids drifted open. "Great. Tired, but great."

He seemed ready to drift off to sleep, but she didn't want to lose the tentative connection they'd formed. Not yet.

"Hey, I've been meaning to ask you." She nipped at the stubble on his chin. "What's your real name?"

He frowned. "What? You know my name."

"Not the name on your birth certificate. Obviously, you weren't born Royce."

He let out a long sigh and shook his head. "Where did this come from?"

She laughed. "Haven't you ever heard the saying about curious cats?"

"And what happens to the curious cat in the saying?"

She rolled her eyes. "It dies. But satisfaction brings it back."

"Sweetheart, if you aren't satisfied by now there's something seriously wrong with you."

"Believe me. I'm satisfied." She pinched his side with her nails and he grimaced. "That's not what I mean and you know it. I want to know about you."

"Okay, okay. Fine. It's not the most interesting story, though. Renaldo Alberto Cardoso is the name my mother gave me when I was born. Royce..." his voice trailed off for a little while and he looked away before finishing. "An old lover I had in Europe years ago told me I look like a Royce. The nickname stuck. I've used it off and on over the years."

She leaned over him and rested her chin on his chest, cocking her head to the side as she studied his face. "Royce, huh? You don't really look like a Royce to me. It seems too stuck-up. I see you with something less pretentious, like Brick or Snake."

He burst out laughing and tugged at one of her curls. "Snake? I'll have to keep that in mind the next time I'm in need of a name change. You've got to admit, though, Royce is a lot better than Renaldo."

"You've got a point there." She rested her head back on his chest, tracing his abs with her fingertips. "Where did you meet Wil?"

"I've known him for too many years to count. We knew each other, years ago, back in Europe. We're a lot alike in some ways."

"You don't seem that much alike to me."

He smiled and kissed the top of her head. The tenderness of his actions struck her and she had to tamp down the fluttering in her heart. "We have our differences. He's a lot more settled than I am."

"I've noticed. The whole house and job thing kind of clued me in."

"Hey! I work."

"Yeah, at nothing."

He shook his head. "I don't like to stay in once place for long. I think Wil's sick of moving around. Me, I couldn't handle a small town like this. I prefer the city. It's so much easier to blend in with the crowd."

Blend? Was he kidding? "A six-foot-four, two-hundred-forty pound blond guy is a little hard to miss anywhere."

An uncomfortable thought hit her and she stopped asking questions. Why was she so anxious to learn about his life? Her curiosity, in this situation, could signify trouble. Trouble of the soon-to-be broken heart kind— something she refused to set herself up for.

She started to doze off in his arms, half-hoping she wouldn't fall in love with him. That would be just plain crazy, and quite possibly the stupidest thing she'd ever done.

Chapter Ten

Merida tried to curl up in Royce's arms and sleep, but she only accomplished a lot of tossing and turning. After a frustrating half hour of listening to Royce breathe as he slept deeply, she heaved herself out of bed, got dressed, and wandered downstairs. He might need sleep, but she needed breakfast. And coffee. Lots of it, if she planned to make it through the day.

As she reached the bottom of the back stairs, the aroma of freshly brewed coffee hit her hard. Her stomach clenched with longing. Did she smell bacon? She dug her fingers into her arm, her nails sharply biting the skin. Nope, not dreaming. Then who...?

She turned the corner into the darkened kitchen. The curtains had been drawn closed over the windows, the only light coming from the globe above the sink. Wil stood by the stove. She leaned against the doorframe and wondered if all the sex with Royce had finally turned her brain to much. Was she hallucinating?

"Good morning," he said before she had a chance to speak.

"How did you know I was in the room?"

"Your presence. It's strong." He turned and smiled at her, and for the first time she saw him as something other than a grump. "I hope you like bacon and eggs."

"Scrambled or fried eggs?"

"Fried."

She let out a deep sigh. "Perfect."

"Sit down. This is just about ready."

She took a seat at the table and Wil set a large stoneware mug in front of her. "Do you need milk or sugar?"

Okay. Someone had broken Royce's friend. "Why are you being so nice to me?"

He shrugged as he set a heaping plate of eggs and bacon in front of her. "Do you want toast?"

This had to be some kind of joke. Either that or she'd tripped and fallen into another dimension. "No, thanks. I'm all set. I have to ask. You didn't poison this, did you?"

He laughed as he slid into the chair across from her. "Why would you ask that?"

"Gee, I wonder." She gestured to the plate of food in front of her. It smelled delicious, but she wanted to know what had caused him to cook for her before she enjoyed it.

He, like Royce, seemed to be adept at reading her mind. "It's going to get cold if you don't eat. I'd imagine, after last night and then this morning, you must need to refuel."

She snapped her gaze from the tempting food to Wil's dark eyes. "What do you know about this morning?"

"Only that the two of you don't feel the need to be quiet."

Her face must have flushed, because he laughed. "No need to be embarrassed. I know that what you and Royce have is—"

She held up her hand to stop him before he went too far and assumed things that weren't true. Mostly weren't true, at least not while she was still in the denial stage.

"We have nothing. This food smells great. Thanks."

She picked up her fork and started to eat, doing her best to ignore Wil's presence. He sat across from her, unmoving and unsmiling and making her want to strangle him. Halfway through the meal she couldn't take the tense silence anymore. "Okay. What's going on?"

"What do you mean?"

"Face it. You're a man. You wouldn't have cooked me breakfast, especially since you don't eat this kind of food, if you didn't want something."

"I don't mind cooking. Really."

She leaned on the table, eyebrows raised, and glared at him until he relented. "I cooked for you because I wanted to. And because I have something to run by you. I was hoping you'd be down here when I got home, but you and Royce were...busy and I had to do something to kill time before I fell asleep."

She pushed the plate away, took a long sip of her coffee and leaned back in the chair. "What's the problem?"

"I don't know if it is a problem, but a gut feeling tells me it might be."

She listened while he explained the conversation he'd had with Michelle earlier that morning. By the time he finished, her suspicions were raised. "Did you know about any of this sooner?"

He shook his head. "I'd never bothered to check."

Meaning Michelle hadn't been that important to him for him to learn even the little facts about her upbringing. Men. She sighed. Vampires. It seemed they were all alike. "Here's a question for you. Michelle's dad has been dead for years, right?"

"Yes."

"Then if he sold out to a demon, the contract would have dissolved with his death."

"Yeah, I get that. But how do you explain what she told me?"

"Coincidence." She shrugged and took another gulp of coffee, feeling the caffeine start to kick in. Another ten cups of this stuff and she'd be good to go. "That's all I can offer you right now. Unless you think Michelle is the one who made the deal."

Wil stood up and stretched before removing his tie and unbuttoning the first couple buttons of his navy blue dress shirt. "I doubt it. She thought her mother was nuts for even saying anything about the devil."

She closed her eyes and pinched the bridge of her nose. She didn't know if there was any truth to Wil's theory about Michelle and her father, but she knew how to find out. She just had to get rid of a well-meaning but controlling vampire first. "You look tired. Maybe you should go to bed."

"I'm going. I just wanted to run all this by you first."

"I'm glad you did, but I don't think there's anything to worry about. Goodnight," she added as he left the kitchen. She heard his footsteps on the stairs a few seconds later and silently cursed him for not bothering to do the dishes. Men, no matter what their race, were all the same. She supposed she'd have to do them, but it would have to wait until later. She had her first semi-decent lead since arriving in Caswell, and she had no plans to let it slip away.

When she heard Wil's door close she crept up the stairs and peeked into her bedroom. Royce lay flat on his back, his eyes closed and his lips slightly parted. Her fingers itched to trace the line of stubble along his jaw, her mouth ached to kiss his warm lips, his broad chest, his washboard abs, his—

"Stop it!" she whispered to herself. If she went any lower with her imaginary kisses, she'd never get her job done. Assured that he slept soundly, she walked into his room and rummaged through his black duffel bag until she found his car keys. He thought he could hide them from her. She would have laughed out loud at the idea if she hadn't been afraid to wake up the bloodsuckers.

She picked up a navy blue zip front sweatshirt out of the bag and put it on, hoping it would help ward off some of the chill she knew she'd feel from the evil presence where the murders occurred. Five minutes later, she pulled Royce's car out of the driveway and headed toward town.

She cranked up the radio and opened the windows, letting the warm breeze whip through her hair. She'd never figure out how the two of them could sleep during the day and not miss seeing all of this. She'd never be able to handle being a day sleeper. She loved the sun, the fresh air too much. That thought put a damper on her good mood. Just one more thing she and Royce didn't have in common.

She wanted to take his advice, to go with whatever happened between them and not worry about labels, but everything reminded her of their differences. What did they really have in common? Besides incredible chemistry in the bedroom, nothing. At least she didn't think so. She didn't know much about him. What she knew, she liked— which is why she'd stopped asking questions. She didn't *want* to like him. She didn't want to care about him at all.

But she did.

Why, she had no clue. She didn't generally gravitate toward chauvinistic cavemen who only thought of themselves and only dated weak women with no minds of their own. So why Royce? Why now, when she was just starting over and trying to get her life together? She could only come up with one answer. Temporary insanity.

Or maybe PMS. Didn't women get away with anything for that? It would explain why she couldn't seem to keep her hands off him, even knowing what kind of man he was. She didn't know. Not really. She knew what she saw — what he let the world see. She had a feeling, though, that he kept his true self hidden deep inside and didn't let many people in. Ellie couldn't say enough nice things about him. But Ellie didn't have a bad word to say about anyone. She ran a hand through her hair and tried to tuck it back behind her ears. When the wind whipped it back over her face within seconds, she growled in frustration. Why did she spend so much time thinking about a dead-end fling when she had a job to do?

She stopped the car down the street from the duplex in case Michelle happened to be home. The last thing she needed now was a bunch of irritating questions. She couldn't stand reporters. She shut the car door softly and walked down the soft roadside to the front door. It swung open with no effort this time and she walked inside.

"Hello?" she called, not expecting an answer.

She nearly jumped out of her skin when she got one. "I've been expecting you."

She shivered at the scratchy, nails on a chalkboard quality of the voice echoing through the room. "Who's there?" Glancing around the dark apartment, she saw nothing more sinister than the shadows in the corners.

Out of those shadows crept a small round figure cloaked in black. "I know what you are." He raised his head slowly and met her gaze with glowing orange eyes.

His grayish wrinkled face and sunken mouth sent a chill up her spine. She'd seen a lot of things, but nothing like this. Demons usually fell into two categories—the kind from late-night horror movies that scared the pants off average people, and the kind like her, who could take on a human form and disappoint horror fans everywhere. This thing...he didn't look like a monster. He looked like death, desolation, desertion. A complete void of anything happy and loving. Her worst nightmare. She drew a fortifying breath before facing him. "That's great. So you're at an advantage, because I have no idea what you are. It seems to me that, in a fair fight, I should at least have an idea of what kind of a being you are."

"*Aparasei.*"

The word was no more than a harsh whisper from his lips, but it chilled her to the bone. *Aparasei.* She'd heard that name a few times in her life, always in a hushed whisper. *Aparasei* were beings even the strongest demons feared. She'd always been warned to stay away from them—which usually ended up being a moot point since they very rarely left the demonic plane to invade the world of humans.

"What are you doing here?" she asked, not sure if she really wanted to hear the answer.

"I came to collect what is mine."

Her stomach bottomed out at his confession. She had to struggle to keep her voice even as she spoke. "And what would that be?"

"All things in time. Why are you here, little cat?" He stepped toward her, his gait uneven as he hunched over an ancient-looking brown gnarled cane. The cane base thumped hollowly against the floor with each step the *Aparasei* took.

Instinct kicked in and she backed up a few steps. To let the thing touch her would be to cause her own death. "To help a friend."

"A noble intention. Yet, is it your only motive?"

"What are you talking about?"

"You had no wishes to help a man you would not have considered a friend," he told her, his haunting gaze locking with hers. "You wished to run away from a destiny that has been yours since birth, Merida."

The conversation had officially moved beyond creepy. "How do you know my name?"

"I know many things about you. The *Aparasei* have a special interest in the lives of Balance Keepers."

"I am *not* a Balance Keeper."

He cocked its head to the side and gave her a ghastly smile full of broken orange teeth. "Oh, no? I beg to differ."

She shook her head. "I don't want that. If you're planning to try to get rid of me because of some ridiculous destiny, you're wasting your time. I turned it down."

His laugh made her stomach clench. "You cannot just say no. Your destiny doesn't work that way. I can help you, though, if you wish."

She crossed her arms over her chest and raised her eyebrows. "How?"

"We can trade, a favor for a favor."

A favor. She blinked, remembering what Wil had said.

Could Michelle have made some kind of a bargain with the *Aparasei*? "No, thanks. I'm all set. I'll figure it out on my own."

He laughed softly, his eyes glowing even brighter. "I have watched you all your life, little one. I know you are strong. But that won't matter now. One cannot fight one's destiny."

She'd heard that before. From Sam. What she wouldn't give to have Sam with her now, to translate what this wacko was saying. "Let me get this straight. You're here to take some unknown object that you claim is yours. I'm here to help a friend who you seem to think I don't consider a friend. I don't want my destiny, but the only way to get out of it is to make a deal with you. Please tell me I'm not the only one who thinks that's seriously messed up."

He blinked his big eyes and smiled again. "*Messed up* or not, little cat, that is where we stand."

"Which is where? I'm having a little trouble following this conversation."

"We are here for different reasons, yet the same."

She resisted the urge to roll her eyes. The fear she'd first felt had ebbed a little, pushed aside by her annoyance at the thing's penchant for speaking in riddles. "Are you talking about the murders? Did you kill those people?"

He nodded slowly.

"Why? Did they steal the object you think is yours?"

His wide shoulders lifted in a shrug. "They saw me. It was too soon, I hadn't been able to take back what belongs to me. I couldn't let them ruin my chances. I will fulfill my own destiny before the next moonrise. Then I will be gone from this terrible little town. Provided we can agree on an equitable compromise."

"What?" Instead of speaking more clearly, he'd only gotten worse.

"We both need something. I need what has belonged to me for many years, and you need a shift of fate to change your life path. If you must promise to let me retrieve my belongings without interruption from you, I will help you shift your fate."

"Not in a million years, buddy. I have a job to do. I'll find a way to shift my own fate, thanks." She stepped toward him, not sure of what she needed to do but knowing something had to be done. "I can't just let you walk away. You murdered two people. You're a danger to the human world."

"You do not understand," he told her, a menacing smile on his face. "Your fate shifted the second you walked into this house today. I had hoped not to hurt you, but you've given me no choice." He swiped a hand out, catching her across the side of her arm. She felt a terrible stinging, burning sensation that overpowered everything, and then she only saw darkness.

* * * * *

Royce woke up a while after the sunset, blinking as his eyes adjusted to the unfamiliar surroundings. Something soft had tangled around his wrist. He sat up and pulled it off. Merida's stocking—or at least what was left of it after she fried it with her hands. His semi-erect cock tightened in response. That morning had been better than he ever would have expected, a turning point in the relationship neither of them would claim to want.

Where was she?

He hadn't really expected her to hang around wasting the day while he slept, but he'd been hoping she might have come back to bed once the sun went down. Something felt wrong, though. The house seemed too quiet.

He pulled himself out of bed and put his boxers and jeans back on before heading down the stairs to the living room. His heart raced and his nerves tingled. Where was Merida? Something had happened to her. He wasn't sure how he knew, but he did.

When he hurried through the living room door, he stopped short. She sat on the couch, her knees curled up to her chest, her arms wrapped around her legs. She looked pale and tired, but she looked alive. "Hi," he said softly as she looked up at him.

"Hi." Her voice sounded small and weak and it came too close to tearing his heart out. She gave him a tiny smile that did nothing to ease his fears.

"What happened?" he asked, trying to swallow past the lump in his throat.

"I went back to the house."

Anger welled in him and he clenched his fists. Why had she not listened when he and Wil told her it wasn't safe? "Were you trying to get yourself killed? You told me yourself it wasn't safe. You said there was a demon involved."

She shook her head. "It's not a demon. It's an *Aparasei*."

Royce snapped his mouth shut, all thoughts of what he'd planned to say leaving him. He knew she was tough, but she looked so small, so frail. At nearly a foot smaller than him, he couldn't imagine her being strong enough to take on anything as powerful as an *Aparasei*.

"Don't worry. I'm okay," she told him as she stood up from the couch and walked the few steps to him. She surprised him by wrapping her arms around his neck.

His hand automatically went to her back and pulled her closer. "What's wrong?" He rubbed his hand up the side of her arm and pulled away from her when she flinched. "What happened to you?"

She moved her t-shirt sleeve out of the way to reveal a long, thin red welt. At the sight of it, he wanted to go out and find the *Aparasei* that hurt her and tear the thing's head off.

"It's no big deal," she told him, her voice a little stronger. "I'm feeling a lot better now that I've had a chance to rest. At least I didn't hit my head on anything when I fell." Her laugh sounded strangled.

"What do you mean, when you fell? Did he push you?"

She shook her head, her smile not reaching her eyes. "No. When he touched me, I blacked out. I woke up and I had this on my arm."

"Does it hurt?"

"Only when someone touches it. It's starting to go away. I was a lot worse when I woke up."

He pulled her back against him again and kissed the top of her head. If he'd lost her... "When did you wake up?"

"About five hours ago."

"And you've been sitting here the whole time?"

She ducked out of the circle of his arms and walked to the window, giving him her back. "I slept for most of it.

I've only been awake for a little while."

"Then why didn't you come back to bed?"

She turned slowly, and walked toward him, stopping a few feet away. With her hands on her hips and her eyebrows raised, she looked, for the most part, back to the Merida he knew and lo—liked. "I didn't think it would be right to disturb your sleep. After all the sex we had, I thought you might need it."

"Okay. Fine. Can you at least explain to me why you decided to go against your promise to me, and to Wil, and go back to that house? Where you got attacked by something worse than a demon?"

She frowned, her eyes fiery again—just the way he liked them. The tension he'd felt when he woke up finally dissolved.

"I felt like it, okay? You're not my boss." She tried to push past him but he grabbed her around the waist and pulled her back, kissing her hard before she had a chance to protest. He had her panting and clutching at his arms by the time he broke the kiss.

"Do you want me to make you something to eat?"

She blinked up at him, her eyes glazed over, for a couple seconds before the lust-filled gaze turned to a glare. "Are you crazy? Do you really think I'm going to take a meal from a man who hasn't cooked anything in a few hundred years?"

Yep. She was back to her old self. He smiled.

"I only ate what Wil cooked for me this morning because I was starved."

His smile faded. "Wil cooked for you?"

"Well, yeah. I assumed you knew." She shrugged and

walked past him. He followed her into the kitchen. She grabbed a twin pack of granola bars and sliced open the package with her fingernail. "Is there a problem?"

"Why would you let Wil cook for you?"

"It wasn't like I had a choice." She rolled her eyes and bit off another chunk of granola bar. "I woke up. He'd already cooked. What was I supposed to do?"

Royce was about to answer when someone banged on the front door. "Hold that thought. We are definitely not done here." Not wanting Wil to wake up before they finished their conversation, he walked to the front door and swung it open. A tall, dark-haired woman stood there. She smiled when she saw him, her blue eyes flashing interest. "Well, hello."

He didn't have to ask to know who she was. "Can I help you?"

"I'm Michelle. I'm looking for Wil." Her smile widened, displaying a row of gleaming white teeth. He had the passing thought that they couldn't be real—nothing that perfect ever was. "Maybe he's mentioned me?"

"He's sleeping."

Royce whirled to see Merida standing a few feet behind him, her face expressionless.

Michelle's expression shifted from interested to annoyed. And maybe a little jealous. "He asked me to meet him here tonight. Could someone possibly go and get him for me?"

She pushed past Royce and walked into the house, stopping in front of Merida. "Who are you people?"

Merida shrugged. "Wil's friends."

"Friends? Do you *friends* have names?"

Royce stepped between them before Michelle got hurt. If she kept badgering Merida, she'd end up with more than a few scratches. "I'm Royce, and that's Merida."

Michelle beamed up at him. "I've heard about you. A few times, in fact. Wil can't say enough good things about you." She turned her gaze back toward Merida and frowned. "But Wil hasn't mentioned *your* name."

One corner of Merida's mouth lifted into a half-smile and her eyes took on a dangerous expression. "Give it time. We just met."

Michelle blinked but said nothing.

Merida's smile widened. "I'll go wake Wil up. Stay here." She turned and left the kitchen.

Michelle shook her head. "She's a little odd, isn't she?"

"No." What the hell did she think she was doing, going up to Wil's bedroom alone? If she wasn't back in five minutes, he'd have to kick some serious ass.

* * * * *

"What were you thinking, coming here when you knew I was in bed?" Wil glared at Michelle, ready to put his fist through a wall. He'd been woken out of a much needed sleep to find she'd shown up without notice, trying to cause problems. "It's bad enough that you use me for information. Did you really have to come in here and harass my friends?"

For once, she had the decency to look wounded. "I didn't come here to bother anyone. I just wanted to see you."

Yeah. *Right.* A few weeks ago, he might have believed that. But that was before he'd gotten to know her. She might have the rest of the world fooled, but she didn't care about anything but her own aspirations. She'd proven to him that she'd do whatever it took to get information out of him, including feeding him that story about her father's murder. He'd looked into it before going to bed that morning. There hadn't been a murder. In fact, there was question that her father was even dead. From what Wil had read, it appeared Dale Silverman had cleaned out the company bank accounts and disappeared, leaving his business partner with nothing. So why had Michelle lied?

Because she was just like her father. Ruthless, uncaring, only looking out for herself. He took in her perfect hair and clothes, her impeccable makeup—her attitude. He shook his head. She sucked everybody in with her sob stories. He regretted ever falling for any of them. "Go home, Michelle. I'll call you later."

"No you won't. We need to have a talk. *Now.*"

He faced her, his arms crossed over his chest. "What do you want now?"

"What's happening to us? I just don't feel like we're close anymore. We could have it all, if you'd just let me in. But there's something wrong with you. You barely socialize, you stay inside most of the time, and you work too much. You don't eat when we go out. You never drink anything besides water." She frowned. "You know what? You barely qualify as human."

He sucked in a sharp breath and let it out on a sigh. "That's the most ridiculous thing I've ever heard. Not everyone needs to comply with your standards of normal."

"Normal? Wil, your behavior is strange by any standards."

"If you came to berate me for my lifestyle, go home. I don't need to conform to your warped views of conventional."

She put her hand on his arm, not noticing when he tried to flinch away. "I'm sorry. I've been going through a lot of stress right now. You have, too. Why don't we do something about that? Let's take a vacation."

"Are you out of your mind?"

Her voice took on a high, almost desperate tone. "Wil, please. Listen to me. We should run away together, just the two of us. Go to some tropical island and sit in the sun all day. We could live there. We wouldn't ever have to come back."

Yeah, that would do him a lot of good. It'd probably kill him in a week. "And how do you suggest we support ourselves?"

"You've got plenty—" She snapped her mouth shut, but he didn't need her to say any more to know what she'd done.

"You've been snooping into my finances."

She glanced around the room, growing more skittish by the second. "I'm sorry."

"How did you manage it?" He grabbed her arms when she tried to hurry out of the room, turning her around roughly. "Tell me, Michelle."

She stared up at him, her eyes filled with fear. "Jake Brighton at the bank. I used to date him."

"Jake Brighton." He had a feeling it wasn't as over as she pretended. "I think you need to leave."

"That's right! We both need to leave. Let's go together."

"No. I don't think so. You need to get out of this house before I do something I'll regret."

"You love me," she said forcefully, as if telling him so would make it true. He shook his head.

"No, I don't. I was very clear on that from the beginning."

A panicked expression took over her face. "You can help me, Wil. I need you. I need your help."

"I don't think so."

"You're going to be sorry. I can promise you that." Her foot caught on a chair leg as she turned to run, knocking her to the floor. She jumped up before he could help her, rubbing her elbow. "Look at what you made me do."

She pulled her hand away from her elbow and lifted it inches from his face, her fingertips bloodied. Wil's gut clenched at the sight of the blood. Something he usually kept control over snapped inside him. How he wanted to taste it, to feel it running over his tongue… He shook his head and turned away before she saw that his fangs had started to elongate. "You'd better leave, Michelle. Now."

"You can't get rid of me that easily."

He turned to her, rage and hunger overpowering everything else. "Fine. Don't. But I can't promise I won't hurt you."

Her eyes widened and she stumbled back a few steps. "Your teeth…they're…what the hell is wrong with you?"

"Haven't you ever heard of vampires?" He advanced on her, backing her into the wall next to the door.

She shook her head furiously, her face going pale. "No. It's not possible. There's no such thing as vampires."

He lifted her slack wrist in his hand and brought it to within inches of his mouth. "I can prove otherwise."

She jerked her hand away and put her palms on his chest, shoving hard. He didn't move much, but enough that she could slide past him and hurry out of the kitchen. Chest heaving, stomach clenching in hunger, he chased her to the door. She was quick, though, and he didn't catch her as she ran down the rain-covered front steps and jumped into her car.

As he listened to her car peel away, he sunk back against the doorframe, cursing himself for his lack of control. She'd tell everyone what had happened. Even if no one believed the vampire story, she could still file assault charges. In one moment, he'd just ruined his entire life.

Chapter Eleven

Not long after Merida and Royce had left the house to give Wil some privacy, it had started to rain. The warmth in the air combined with the fat drops of rain felt refreshing after the terrible morning she'd had. She lifted her face toward the sky, eyes closed, letting the cool water wash over her.

"Maybe we should go inside," Royce said. "You're not in top form and I don't want you to get sick."

She pushed away his hand when he tried to lead her back to the house. "Don't be silly. I love the rain."

"I thought cats didn't like water."

"Housecats, maybe. I love it." She turned to him leaned up and kissed him. "Are you afraid of getting wet? Afraid you'll melt?"

"I know I won't. But I worry about you."

"Well, don't. I need this. I need to forget what happened earlier." The *Aparasei* and its touch lingered at the back of her mind. She couldn't push it away, no matter how much she tried, but she didn't want to think about it right now. "Want to help me forget?"

"I don't want to hurt you."

"So don't," she told him before she pulled him down for another kiss.

After a few seconds, Royce pulled back. He stared down at her, worry in his eyes. "Are you sure about this? Your arm."

"My arm is fine." She lifted the sleeve of her shirt and showed him. The red welt had faded to a light pink, shiny raised scar. "I don't know if this'll ever go away, but the pain is gone."

Royce ran his finger gently over the scar. "I'm sorry."

"You didn't do it."

"I brought you here." He sighed and turned away, walking a few steps across the yard. "You could have been killed."

Did he think she was some helpless twit? "Listen, Macho Man. I'm fine. Obviously. I wouldn't have gone into the situation if I thought I'd risk my life." *Liar.* "I don't take risks like that."

He turned slowly, his hands shoved in the pockets of his faded jeans. "I should be protecting you. None of that should have happened."

"Knock it off." She watched him closely as a myriad of emotions played across his chiseled features—regret, anger, sadness—anything but the lust and desire she wanted, *needed* to see. He shook his head and turned away again, facing the woods at the edge of the yard, his shoulders shaking with emotion. Didn't he get it? She didn't want this kind of emotion. Not from him.

And then it hit her. Everything slid into place and she realized why he was acting the way he was. She walked up to him and punched him in the arm. "What the hell is wrong with you?"

Taken aback, Royce glared at her. "What are you talking about?"

"I'm not your wife."

He opened his mouth, but snapped it shut again before he spoke. He ran a big hand through his hair, slicking the wet strands back from his face, as his expression darkened. When he finally responded, his angry tone made her stomach clench. "I'm well aware of that. No one in their right mind would ever compare you to Sarah." He shook his head and started to walk back toward the house.

"Where are you going?" she taunted. "Just like you to run away when things get too personal."

He spun and stalked back toward her, his hands clenched into fists at his sides and his blue eyes so dark they looked almost black. "Where do you get off talking to me like that? I told you before and I'll say it again—you don't know me. You don't want to know me, kitty, so I suggest you back off."

"No."

His eyes widened and his nostrils flared. He let out a harsh breath. "What the fuck are you trying to do?"

"I'm trying to get you to face your emotions, for once in your life. You've been shut off from the rest of the world for so long you don't even know how to open yourself up. I'm trying to be your friend. Every time I think you're starting to let me in, you pull this shit and push me away again."

"*I* didn't push *you* away. *I* didn't start this. You did, by even thinking I'd make the mistake of comparing you to my wife."

She opened her mouth, but he held a hand up to keep her from speaking. He continued his tirade, stepping closer until she started backing across the yard. "There is nothing similar between you and Sarah. *Nothing.* Sarah was soft and sweet. Most of the time, you're a nasty bitch. Sarah never talked back to me. You seem to get off on it."

He drew another deep breath and let it out on a shuddering sigh, backing her against the metal shed in the corner of the small yard. He stopped inches from her, not touching but still crowding her with his big body, his intense presence. She gulped. Maybe provoking him hadn't been the best idea.

"Okay, you've made your point. Sarah was wonderful. I'm not. End of discussion." She tried to duck away, but he grabbed her wrists and pinned them to the cold metal, next to her head.

"We're not even close to done here." He leaned in, his heated breath feathering across her cheek. She shivered from the cold, from fear of what he could do to her, and from the arousal he stirred in her just from being so close—so in her face. "You really should think before you open your mouth. Your impulsiveness is going to lead to a lot of hurt someday, kitty."

She nodded, squirming under the intensity in his gaze. "I'm sorry if I—"

"*Sorry?* Do you think I'm stupid? You're never sorry." He barked a bitter laugh. "You know what? That's what you and Sarah have in common."

"What?" she asked, her voice shaky. She'd never seen him like this, and she didn't know if she liked it. Her pussy dampened at his forcefulness in the same way it had when he'd tied her up and spanked her. It shook her to think something like *this* would turn her on.

"She screwed me over. Left me for my brother. Made me not want to feel again. *Ever.*" Royce's breathing grew jagged and his hands shook as he held her wrists to the side of the shed. He pressed closer, his body less than an inch from hers. "You...you're worse. You took the numbness away. You made me *feel* again. And now you continue to rub salt in the wounds you reopened. You're going to leave me raw."

"Sarah and I aren't that much alike," she told him. "I'm still here. I'm not going to leave you for someone else." She wanted to bite back the words as soon as they left her mouth. She didn't want to promise him things she wasn't ready to keep.

"It's not the same." He shook his head, spraying cold water over her face. "*I'm not in love with you.*"

She sucked in a breath at his too-vigorous declaration. "Who are you trying to convince?"

"*No one,*" he growled, and from the look in his eyes, she knew he lied. Desperate to change the direction of their concentration, she pushed against his hands with her wrists.

"Fine. No one ever said this was about love. We're using each other, right? A little mutual satisfaction. So how about it? Why don't you let me go and we can satisfy each other."

"Sounds like a plan to me. I'm in the mood to be used." He dropped his hands to her sides and, without giving her time to react, pulled her against him, and crushed his lips to hers. His kiss was demanding, dominating—devastating to her senses. His clean masculine scent filled her lungs, his taste hot in the mouth. He pressed her into the shed, lifting her legs around his hips and grinding his rigid cock against her. She cried out as he bit her lip, his fangs puncturing her flesh. Her body went boneless and she dug her nails into his shoulders to keep from sliding to the ground.

He broke the kiss and let her go. Her feet hit the

ground and her knees almost gave out. She tried to grab onto Royce for support, but he backed away a step. "Take off your jeans and panties."

"Excuse me?"

"Take them off before I rip them off. I don't think you want to walk back into the house and parade around naked in front of Wil and his girlfriend. Lose the pants, Merida. *Now.*"

Oh God. Her cunt quivered at his harsh, raw tone. Her legs barely able to hold her, she unzipped her jeans and dragged the heavy, wet fabric down her legs. Her panties followed and she dropped the soaked clothes into a pile on the grass. She started to lift her shirt over her head, but Royce wouldn't let her. "Don't bother," he told her as he pushed her back against the shed.

He unzipped his own jeans and freed his cock, rubbing the head over her aching pussy. "Don't tease," she moaned.

He laughed. "Teasing isn't want I have in mind right now." He grabbed her ass in his hot, damp palms and pulled her up higher, thrusting his cock into her cunt, all the way to the hilt. He was huge and so hard she almost couldn't take it. She cried out and wrapped her arms around his neck to steady herself as he pumped into her. His thrusts were vicious, primal, feeding her lust on a level she hadn't experienced in too long to remember. She lost herself in the feel of him, the way he moved against her so perfectly right. It had never been like this for her, and she knew it never would be again. She'd never find a man to satisfy her the way Royce did.

It shook her to think that he satisfied her in an emotional sense as well as a physical one. She tried to push the thought out of her head, but it wouldn't budge. If she didn't control her emotions, she would fall in love with the guy. What a disaster that would be.

He ground his pelvis against her in a way that had her forgetting why any of that would be a bad idea. She could barely even remember her name. Her orgasm took her by surprise, slamming into her with the force of a hurricane and causing just as much damage. Her mind spun, her muscles clenched and slackened, her ears buzzed. Her heart swelled and ached, knowing she needed him but she'd never fully have him. He'd devoted his life to one woman—a woman who had walked away from him and destroyed his soul. He kept his heart so guarded now that she would never be able to get close. It hurt, but she'd get over it. She'd have to.

She collapsed against Royce, her head falling to his shoulder as he stiffened and came inside her. Much too soon he set her down on her feet. He bent down and picked up her clothes, handing them to her with too much regret in his eyes. "Here."

"Thanks." She turned away to dress, hoping he hadn't seen the tears welling in her eyes.

* * * * *

"You're losing it, buddy," Wil told Royce as he walked into the living room an hour later.

"Yeah. No shit." After a long, hot shower and good deal of time pacing the bathroom floor, he'd come to a realization. He'd been a complete asshole to Merida. She hadn't deserved any of what he'd said to her. She'd been wrong to try to press him to talk to her, but it hadn't been necessary for him to go off on her like that, either. "I don't know what's wrong with me. I'm letting my control slip a little too much lately."

"Ya think?" Wil shook his head as he flipped through the TV channels. "You could have hurt her out there."

"No. I never would have—wait a second. You saw?"

"Yeah. After Michelle, um, left, I went looking for you. I almost told you to cut the crap and stop scaring her, but I figured you would have tried to beat the shit out of me."

He nodded in agreement. "I didn't scare her, though."

"Yes, you did." Wil turned the TV off and glanced at Royce. "I saw it in her eyes. She looked ready to pass out for a minute there."

Royce narrowed his eyes at Wil. "How much did you see?"

"I watched you pull your caveman act, pinning her to the shed like some kind of prey. I left after that."

Royce let out a sigh of relief. Merida would kill him if she thought Wil had been watching.

"She deserves better than you," Wil told him, his expression darkening.

"Yeah, like I don't know that already." Royce leaned back against the couch cushions and closed his eyes, drawing a deep, shaky breath. His body had yet to recover from the way Merida broke him down every time they touched. She *did* deserve better, but he couldn't stay away. He'd been fooling himself if he'd really thought having her under him again would make him forget about her. Her willingness to do whatever he asked, at least sexually, surprised him—but it also branded his mind with her presence. There would be no forgetting. At least not in this lifetime.

"But you aren't going to let her go, are you?" Wil asked.

"The hell I'm not." Royce sat up and snapped his eyes open, the muscles in his shoulders bunching at the thought of letting her walk away again, but he didn't have a choice. She'd do it, and he'd let her. That was how it was supposed to be. "She doesn't want me. We'll get sick of each other soon, and then we'll go our separate ways. We're just having fun."

"Giving in to a little chemistry, huh?" Wil asked, an eyebrow raised.

"That about sums it up."

"That's bull, and we both know it."

Royce glared at Wil, his jaw clenched. "Whatever," he mumbled.

Royce sank into silence as he mulled over Wil's words. He couldn't accept them as the truth. Not yet. Not when he didn't know what she wanted out of the chemistry between them. Probably nothing. He needed something to focus on besides the issues clenching his heart. "Merida had an interesting encounter."

He detailed the events at the duplex as Merida had described them to him. Wil sat in an unnatural silence the entire time. When he finished speaking, Wil shook his head.

"That doesn't sound promising."

Talk about an understatement. "I think it affected her more than she'll admit to. She was a mess when I found her on the couch."

"Can she handle it?" Wil asked, his expression clouded with doubt.

Royce shrugged. "Probably. I have faith in her. If she can't figure it out, she knows some people who can. She's strong-willed, but she's not stupid."

"She's not nuts, either," Wil said softly. Wil shook his head and closed his eyes. When he opened them again, Royce saw the same regret he felt mirrored in Wil's eyes.

Royce frowned. "What happened?"

Wil let out a harsh breath. "She wanted me to go away with her. She was planning to leave Caswell and go to some island in the tropics."

Royce snorted at the thought of a vampire in tropical paradise. "That would have been fun."

"My thoughts exactly. I told her it was over. Again. But she wouldn't listen." He grew silent, his gaze drifting to the other side of the room, his expression flat. "She fell. Cut her arm. She bled, and I snapped."

A cold chill ran through Royce as he thought about the times in the past Wil had snapped. There hadn't been many, but the end results had never been pretty. "What did you do?"

"*Nothing*. Nothing. She ran away before I could hurt her, but I scared her. A lot."

"It sounds like we're both in the same boat."

"Not even close." Wil let out a strained laugh. "Michelle is human. She doesn't understand. She's also a reporter. This is going to turn out bad. Very bad."

"Want me to go talk to her?"

Wil shook his head. "That would just make it worse. I'll handle it, okay? I have to get ready for work. I have to be there in an hour."

"Do you really think it's wise to go in tonight after

what happened?"

"I don't see that I have much choice." Wil's shoulder lifted into a casual shrug, but the dark expression in his eyes had Royce worried. Wil had more than a few skeletons in his closet, ones Royce thought he'd buried long ago. Now, he wasn't so sure. And he didn't like the idea of letting Wil leave in this state.

"Just don't do anything I wouldn't do," Royce told him, only half-joking. He knew about Wil's temper, as much as the guy tried to hide it, and he knew what he was capable of when he got angry. It was definitely something Michelle didn't want to experience firsthand.

After Wil left, Royce went upstairs and ducked his head into Merida's bedroom. How she could sleep after what they'd done—what he'd done to her—he had no idea. But sleep she did, soundly and peacefully. She looked like an angel, bathed in the soft moonlight, her auburn curls fanned across the white pillows in a cascade of fiery locks. His fingers itched to tangle in those incredible strands, to pull her close and kiss her senseless, but he held himself back. She needed her rest, and he needed to work some things out in his head. Everything had changed. He didn't know when it had happened, only that it had. Nothing would ever be the same again. He'd meant what he said to her earlier. When she left him, she'd leave him raw. It would be too much to bear.

He went back downstairs and slipped out the front door, sitting on the porch in the rain. It had started to cool off, leaving the air damp and chilly. He barely noticed the cold. His mind wouldn't let go of Merida, and how incredibly *right* it felt to be around her. She was inside his skin, inside his soul—if he even had one left—and he wanted more.

Did he want to chance everything and go for something lasting? He didn't know. When Sarah had left him, she'd torn his heart out. She'd been his life, his reason for living. But she'd fallen for his brother, a man Royce had thought dead. Marco, his own flesh and blood, had turned Sarah into something he'd thought inconceivable — a vampire. She'd been the cause of Royce's death, of sorts, when he'd turned vampire to win her back. He'd been too late. Sarah had killed herself and left him alone in agony.

But he'd gotten over it. He'd buried it deep, eventually forgetting the pain. He'd been vampire for four hundred years, living life on his terms, not letting another woman close enough to hurt him. One had been enough.

Until Merida.

He kicked his legs up and crossed his ankles on the porch railing, letting the rain hit his bare feet. He was in way too deep with her and he didn't see any possible way to dig himself out.

A small voice in his head — one he chose to ignore — asked him why he even bothered to fight it.

Chapter Twelve

Calusius stood in the corner of the room where the demon woman slept, blissfully unaware in her dream state of the presence of an *Aparasei*. He smiled as he looked at her, so fair for one of her kind. Beautiful. Deceptively peaceful, given her attitude while awake. But she was also too full of herself. She thought she could defeat him? She wouldn't even know where to begin. She had no knowledge of his kind and how it related to hers. He, on the other hand, knew exactly what he was to her.

Her worst nightmare.

He could kill her with ease as she lay there sleeping, but where would the amusement be in that? He wanted a battle. He wanted excitement. He had come to Caswell for the woman promised to him twenty-six years ago, but now he wondered if he might like to take something else back to his dimension as well. A little cat would fit nicely with his…collection, especially one who wasn't afraid to show her claws.

He walked to her bed, his gaze never leaving her face as he made his decision. He would not pass up such an opportunity. When he left Caswell—which would be very soon—he would take two back with him. The little cat wouldn't be left behind.

He stretched his arm out and brushed his fingertips across her cheek. She shuddered in sleep, but did not wake.

"Sleep well, little cat," he told her. "While you still can."

* * * * *

Merida walked across the empty room, the smell of blood strong in the damp, dank air around her. A red glow washed over the walls and the sheet-draped furniture.

A screeching voice greeted her as she approached a darkened doorway on the far side of the room. "Come here, little one."

As if entranced, she walked into the room and found herself face to face with the shadowed figure. The Aparasei. *"What's your name?"*

"Calusius."

"You murdered two people."

He nodded. "I will murder more, those you are close to, if you stand in my way."

"I told you before. I can't let you get away with what you did."

His eyes glowed as he smiled at her. "Ah, the inherent goodness of a Balance Keeper."

"I'm not a Balance Keeper."

"You are correct. Your destiny has shifted." His smile widened and Merida felt sick to her stomach. "I have marked you. That alone changed your life path."

"How is that possible?"

"You will soon find out." He walked around her slowly, his gaze burning into her, making her skin crawl. "When I leave, you will come with me."

"Bullshit." She turned to him, her hands on her hips. "When I'm through with you, there won't be enough left of you to fill an urn."

"You cannot stop me. You will die trying." He lifted his hand to her cheek and stroked his fingertips across her cheekbone. She felt the icy burn where his bony fingers touched her flesh. She tried to scream, but no sound came out.

Merida woke with a start, her body shaking. She bolted upright in bed, gasping for breath and rubbing her hands up and down her arms to warm her chilled body. The room was empty, but she didn't feel it. The *Aparasei's*—Calusius's presence filled the room. It shook her, and she didn't want to be alone.

"Royce?" she called, her voice sounding thin and high. "Royce, are you around?"

A few minutes later, he barged into the room. "What's wrong?"

"I had a bad dream." She blinked as she heard what she said. A bad dream? She felt like she was five. She shook her head, needing to be adult about this. "Do you have a minute? Maybe I can run it by you, and you can tell me what you think."

He shut the door and scooted onto the bed, laying on his side on the mattress and pulling her into his arms. He kissed the top of her head and brushed her hair off her face. "Sure. Tell me what happened."

Being coddled like a baby made her feel foolish. She was almost six hundred years older than him. Why did she like it so much when he treated her this way? She tried to wriggle away, but he held her tight. "Talk to me, Merida. I promise I'll try to help."

"What time is it?"

"Three a.m. Still the middle of the night. I'm wide awake. Tell me about your dream."

He clutched her in the circle of his arms, not in a

sexual way, but one that made her feel safe and warm and protected. Already the anxiety from the dream had started to subside. "It wasn't that bad, really. Not scary, just disturbing."

"How so?" Royce asked softly, sounding like he genuinely wanted to hear what she had to say. It was quite a switch from hours earlier, when he accused her of trying to break him down emotionally.

"I dreamed that I saw the *Aparasei* again. Calusius. In the same house."

"Calusius? How do you know that's his name?"

"Because he told me."

"It was just a dream, honey." He brushed another kiss over the top of her head and she settled back more fully into his warmth.

"It didn't feel like a dream. It felt real." She sighed, realizing how ridiculous she must sound to Royce. "He told me he was going to take the woman promised to him, and that he was going to take me back with him, too."

"Too much stress," Royce told her, pulling her more tightly against him. "Go back to sleep. I've heard that you never dream the same thing twice."

"Not unless it's a prophecy," she mumbled.

He brushed his hand over her cheek and she flinched.

"What's wrong with your face? It's hot. Are you sick?" He turned her head and glanced down at her in the moonlight. His eyes widened. "You have a mark on your face. Did I hurt you earlier?"

"What kind of a mark?" A chill ran down her spine and she tried to brush it off as nothing, even though she knew deep down inside that she was wrong.

"If I didn't know any better, I'd say it looks like fingers." Royce brushed his fingertips over her cheekbone. She winced at the burning sensation his touch caused. "Right here. There are two distinct marks, bright red, like someone burned you with their fingers."

Aparasei. She'd heard that their touch burned flesh, but she'd always passed it off as legend. Now she knew the truth. She pulled out of Royce's arms and jumped out of bed. She picked her small suitcase up from the floor and dropped it onto the bed, digging through it for something to wear. She grabbed a pair of khaki pants and a white tank top, pulling the clothes on over her underwear before searching for her shoes.

"What do you think you're doing?" Royce asked as he climbed out of her bed.

"I have to get out to that house. I can't sit around and wait for him to come to me again." She slipped into her mules, grabbed her gray hooded sweatshirt, and pulled it over her head. "I have to stop him before he hurts someone."

"What makes you think he's going to hurt someone?"

"The dream. Also, I sensed a lot of anger in him when I met him. It overpowered every other emotion. He told me he wanted what belonged to him. I assumed he meant a thing, but he didn't. He meant a person, Royce. An innocent person. I've got to stop him before he does something." She pulled open the door and stepped out in the hall. "You'd better call Wil."

"You think the *Aparasei* wants to hurt Wil?" He sounded incredulous.

She snorted. "I said an innocent person, Royce. I have a funny feeling Wil is even less innocent than you, if that's possible. I'm talking about the people around here who haven't done anything but mind their own business. I have to stop the *Aparasei* before someone else gets killed."

"You can't go alone."

She stopped and turned to him, her hands on her hips. "Why the hell not?"

"Because it isn't safe. Look at what happened the last time you went over their alone."

"I think I can handle myself."

"I don't care. You're not going alone. Not this time." He stepped past her and into his room.

She shot him a dirty look as she watched him pull on his sweatshirt and slip into his boots. "Who do you think you are? What makes you think you can tell me what to do? How can you possibly think you have the right to tell me how to act and where to go?"

He stomped over to her and grabbed her shoulders, shaking her lightly. "Because I love you, that's why." Without giving her a chance to answer, he kissed her hard on the lips before he pushed past her out his bedroom door. "Go use the bathroom or whatever you women have to do when you wake up. I'm going to call Wil and I'll meet you downstairs in five minutes."

"Royce—"

"Downstairs. Five minutes." He started down the back stairs before she could think of a good reply.

She stood there, her fingers to her lips, thinking about what he'd said. He loved her? How could that be possible? He couldn't love her. He couldn't *stand* her. That thought shook her more than it had a right to. He was a vampire, damn it, he didn't deserve a second thought. They had a fling! Nothing else. But she'd seen the truth in his eyes as he'd made his confession. He might not have meant to tell her, but he meant the sentiment behind the words. He loved her.

She tried to shake off the giddy feeling, knowing it would only lead to heartache. So he loved her. *So what?* Who really cared?

She did.

Because she loved him, too.

This was so bad. Terrible. How had she let this happen? She shook her head. Of course, she'd have to put a stop to this foolishness as soon as they'd taken care of the *Aparasei*. They were no good for each other. They couldn't have a civilized conversation without being at each other's throats. One of them would end up dead within a year. So she'd do the only thing she could do when this ended and it was time to go back home. She'd go, and she wouldn't look back. He'd never have to know how much it would break her heart to do so, but they'd both be happier in the end.

Pushing the mushy thoughts out of her mind, she used the bathroom, brushed her teeth, and went downstairs to meet Royce. "I'm all set," she told him as she walked into the kitchen.

He didn't even meet her eyes. "Great. Let's go."

"I called Wil," he told her once they were in his car, his gaze still avoiding hers. "He's going to meet us over there."

"Thank you." She took a deep breath to steady herself before she continued. "About what you said earlier…"

"We aren't going to talk about that right now." He turned the corner onto Magnolia Street and pulled the car up in front of the house. "We'll talk about it later, when everything is over and we're back home. Then we're going to sit down and have a really long, meaningful talk."

She frowned at him. "I didn't think you did long and meaningful."

"I didn't. I'm considering changing my mind. Either that, or I'm losing it. That's probably it. I've finally gone insane." He got out of the car and slammed the door as Wil pulled up behind them. She followed him out of the car.

Wil walked over to them. "Let me see your face."

She pushed the hair away from her cheekbone and he sucked in a sharp breath. "That's not a good thing."

"It looked worse before," Royce told him, glancing first at Merida's cheek and then at the house. "Do you think there's any truth to her dream?"

"Probably, judging from the burn on her face." Wil's expression darkened as he looked at Merida's face.

"Is there something you're not telling me?" she asked him, suspicious at his behavior.

He shook his head. "Nothing of importance. Let's go inside."

The dank, vile-smelling darkness overwhelmed her when they walked through the door. She drew a shaky breath as images from her dream came back to her, and it was all she could do not to run back out the door. She hadn't realized how much the *Aparasei* had frightened her until faced with his scent again.

"It's cold in here," she said softly, closing her eyes against the flood of fear and emotions—none of them good. As she got control of herself, she noticed another scent in the air. She shook her head, thinking her imagination must have kicked into overdrive from the stress. "That's not blood I smell, is it?"

"Yes," Royce whispered. "And it's fresh."

"Shit," Wil said.

She could feel the two of them tense behind her. She reached for the wall switch and flipped on the lights. There, on the white kitchen wall next to them, a message had been written in blood.

"'Let fate take its course, or all three will die,'" she read softly.

"Three?" Wil asked. "What the hell is this all about?"

"It's about us," she whispered, her body chilled to the bone. A cold sweat broke out on her forehead. "I know what he's saying. If you guys don't let him take me back to the demonic plane with him, he'll kill both of you."

"That's not going to happen," Royce said, glancing around the room. "I won't let him hurt you."

"I don't know that you have much choice." She ran a hand through her tangle of curls, slowly losing the battle with stress and nerves. She'd never dealt with a case this personal before. "I've got to figure out a way to defeat him before he hurts anyone else."

"*You* won't be able to do anything about it," Wil said, shaking his head.

She balled her hands into fists at her sides and glared at him. "I've told you before that I can take care of myself."

"I know. But you're missing a pretty big fact here." He gently touched her cheek. "He marked you. Do you know what that means?"

She blinked. "No. Should I?"

"It means you can't do anything to defeat him now.

He's bound you to him."

"*What?*" she and Royce asked at the same time.

"It's the truth. Once you've been marked by an *Aparasei*, you aren't able to destroy one."

Merida narrowed her eyes at him. "How would you know that?"

Wil shrugged. "I've learned a few things in my time." He turned his back before she could ask any more questions, focusing his gaze toward the bloody wall. "What am I going to do about this? I can't very well show this to my chief. Could you imagine his reaction to someone vandalizing the crime scene with blood?"

"I'll take care of it," she told him.

"What are you planning to do? Dig through the cabinets for a bottle of cleaner?"

"Don't be ridiculous. I have a much better way than manual labor." She lifted her hand in the air and made a streaking motion. The blood melted off the wall and dissolved into the air, leaving no trace behind.

Wil blinked. "What the hell was that?"

"That's nothing. Really. It didn't even tax my energy a little."

Wil turned back to her, smiling in open admiration. "Amazing," he said softly. "What else can you do?"

Royce cleared his throat and stepped closer to Merida in a clearly protective—and possessive—gesture. "We should get out of here before someone notices. I'm sure you don't want to answer any questions right now."

"Not really."

"What about the *Aparasei*?" Merida asked. "I need to deal with the problem before—"

"I already told you. You can't." Wil said with a finality that had her gaping. "We'll figure something out."

She had a feeling they wouldn't be able to figure anything out soon enough to stop Calusius's plans.

Chapter Thirteen

Wil slid behind the wheel of his car and watched Royce and Merida drive away into the night. He'd taken his personal vehicle when he'd left work to meet them here because he had no intentions of going back to work. Ever. Things had gotten too complicated, especially with Michelle's knowledge of what he was hanging over his head.

He'd go home later and pack anything he cared about—which didn't amount to much—so he'd be ready. As soon as they found a way to kill the *Aparasei*, he'd be gone. He never stayed in one place long, anyway, and he was pushing the limit in Caswell. Had been for a while. What better time to get out than now?

He watched Michelle's house, looking for signs of life. It was too early, really, for her to be up and getting ready for work, but he couldn't help his curiosity. He needed to speak to her and do some damage control before she filed charges against him—or wrote up an article of what she believed him to be. Suspicions ran high in small towns, especially one as quirky as Caswell. Someone was bound to believe her, and then his life would turn into a witch-hunt. He'd either have to kill or be killed, and neither option suited his current frame of mind.

He shook his head and banged his palms on the steering wheel. Something had to be done about Michelle. When he left a town for good, he never left any loose ends behind. As far as loose ends went, Michelle could be a major problem.

* * * * *

"What is it Wil's not telling me?" Merida asked as they stepped through Wil's front door.

Royce shrugged. There were probably many things Wil kept from her—and all for good reason. He'd doubt any of them related to the case, though. "I have no idea what you're talking about."

"How did he know so much about *Aparasei*? I didn't even know that much and I get rid of beasts like that for a living." She slammed the door and kicked her shoes off, leaving them in the foyer. She stomped into the living room and started pulling the shades down on all the windows.

Royce followed her, his hands stuffed into the pockets of his jeans so he didn't reach out and strangle her. "Careful, Merida, your OCD is showing."

She stopped tugging on the shades long enough to shoot him a scathing glare. "I'm *not* obsessive compulsive. I just don't like the thought that, since the lights are on, someone can see inside."

"There's no one around. Wil doesn't have any close neighbors."

She threw her hands up in the air and heaved a sigh. "You know what? It doesn't matter. I'm not a huge fan of the dark."

When she finished jerking all the shades into place, she flopped down on the couch and let out a shuddering breath. "I need to know what Wil is keeping from me. If he's somehow involved in this mess—"

"Wil isn't involved."

She raised her eyebrows at him. "Are you sure?"

"Positive. He wouldn't have asked me to help him if he'd caused the problem in the first place."

She leaned forward and buried her face in her hands. "Yeah, I suppose you're right," she told him, her voice muffled from her hands. She looked up at him, uncertainty plain in her eyes. "Then I think he might be in a lot of danger. Maybe he should pack up and leave and let me handle things from here."

Oh, yeah. *That* would go over well. "Wil can take care of himself. He doesn't need a woman—"

"Stop right there." She jumped off the couch and stalked over to him, her hands on her hips. "If you go on with that sentence, I'll be forced to kill you."

He glanced down at her, keeping his expression flat. They were all under so much stress, especially after what they'd found tonight, that he wasn't in the mood to be polite. "Go for it. Anything would be better than dealing with you the way you are now."

She narrowed her eyes and punched him in the arm. "Knock it off. I'm serious. I'll hurt you."

"Again, go ahead and try."

She disappointed him when she walked back to the couch and perched on its arm, hugging one knee to her chest while the other leg dangled, her toes barely brushing the beige carpeted floor. Her gaze dropped to the floor and she blew out a breath, blowing her bangs into the air.

Something hitched inside him as he watched her struggle with all that had happened. Her life was in danger and she didn't seem worried at all. Royce knew better, though. He knew a lot of her current attitude resulted from being afraid. She'd never admit her fear, especially not to him, but he felt it in her. He felt it in himself as well, but not for his own life.

For hers.

She was spunky, cute, bitchy, and sexy all rolled into one irresistible package he didn't want to let out of his sight. To say he had tender feelings for her, despite his best intentions, would be a gross understatement. He loved her. He'd meant it when he'd accidentally said the words to her. But that didn't mean he had any plans to say it again anytime soon. Admitting to his feelings would give her power over him, power he couldn't let her have.

Had he made a mistake in letting Merida in when he'd shunned so many others? His mind wanted to say yes, but his heart, just thawing from the deep-freeze he'd kept it in for too many years, knew that would be a lie.

"Uh-oh. You look serious."

"I'm worried about you." The words came out as an automatic reaction—one she didn't care for, if he could judge by the scowl that spread over her face.

"You don't need to be. I've told you that many times before."

"I don't always do things because I need to." He moved over to the couch and sat next to her. She scooted off the arm and paced across the room. "Sometimes, believe it or not, I do things because I want to. I care—"

"No, you don't." She spoke the words softly, but with a force that had him blinking. Did she not want him to care about her?

"Yes, I do. I care about you."

"Well, stop. You're incapable of caring." She shuffled her foot on the floor.

"Maybe you should stop denying everything you feel."

"Maybe you should stop making up things that aren't there." She walked over to the couch and stopped above him, her arms crossed over her chest and a sly smile on her face. "You want to talk? Fine. We'll talk. There's something I've been wanting to ask you for a while, Mr. Sexual Prowess. How many women have you been with at one time?" Merida asked, her nails drawing little designs on his stomach.

"*What?*" That was a switch. He wanted to talk about feelings, and she wanted to talk about sex? "You don't want to know."

She rolled her eyes. "I wouldn't have asked if I didn't want to know. Come on. Tell me. What are you afraid of?"

He laughed. Despite the seriousness of the situation, she'd managed to lighten the mood. "I'm afraid I might ruin my reputation."

"Honey, you can't do any more damage to your reputation. It's already sullied beyond repair. Spill."

With her standing over him, her eyes questioning and her lips slightly parted, his cock tightened. It would take no effort to pull her into his lap. He closed his eyes to ward off the sudden onslaught of lust. Now was not the time to think about sex, not when she had an *Aparasei* trying to take her away. He needed to direct the conversation back to the situation at hand and not the woman too close for his concentration. "A few, okay? Happy now?"

She kicked his foot and cleared her throat. "No. I'm not. I'd appreciate a little honesty. You've been around for a while. I'm sure you've done your share of kinky things."

She had no idea. No one would ever describe him as an angel. Once he'd realized his relative immortality as a vampire, he'd put it to the test in every way possible. "Six."

She didn't say anything for so long he snapped his eyes open to make sure she still stood above him. She gaped at him, her eyes blinking rapidly. "Did I hear you correctly? *Six?* At once? In the same *bed?*"

"Yeah." He waited for her to do something—hit him, call him a pig, stomp out of the room, but she just stood in front of him, shaking her head and muttering under her breath. When she finally spoke, her words shocked him. "How was it?"

"*Hell.* It's hard enough to please one of you. Six was... I don't think I woke up for a week after that one." He smiled up at her, gauging her reaction. She smiled back.

"Are you serious?" At his nod, she laughed. "I thought you men dreamed about that kind of stuff all the time."

"Yeah. We do. It's a great dream. Reality, in that situation, leaves something to be desired." He took her hand and tugged her closer. She stumbled forward but stayed on her feet. "What about you, Merida? Are you into group sex?"

As he said the words, a fire ignited low in his gut. He blew out a breath as his cock pushed against the zipper of his jeans.

"Sorry to disappoint you, Big Guy, but I'm a one-man woman. And before you ask—*only* men. No women."

He tugged her another step closer. "Why not?"

She shrugged. "Never been interested."

"Would you ever change your mind?"

"I'm really not sure." She stepped closer on her own this time, her grip tightening on his fingers. "Why? Are you offering?"

He almost choked. Either his imagination conjured up something he wanted to see in her eyes, or the conversation turned her on. "I'm just asking. That's all. If the opportunity ever arose, would you take it?"

"It would depend on the men, and on the situation. Would you get to be one of the men?"

His cock throbbed at her words. She had to notice how hard she'd made him. If she didn't stop, she'd find herself in big trouble. He wasn't the typical male when it came to sex. He'd found in his years on earth that there were some unusual things he enjoyed. Would she go along with all of them? He gave her hand a sharp tug and she toppled into his lap. "Yeah, I would. If you want me to be."

Her arms came around his neck and she leaned close, her voice a whisper as she spoke. "That would be awesome. Do I get to pick the other guy?"

Fuck.

He drew in a shuddering breath. Was she serious about this? "Sure. Why not?" he answered, his reply strangled as all the blood in his body rushed from his brain to the part currently doing the thinking. She had absolutely no idea what she was getting herself into. In about two seconds, if she didn't stop talking like that, he'd rip her clothes off and take her on the coffee table.

She ran her tongue along the length of his jaw. "Your friend Wil is kind of cute. Think he's up for it?"

Hold on a second. Wil? Jealousy slammed into him, a cold chill washing over his body. He didn't know if he wanted to share the woman he loved. If she wanted to bring in someone else, he'd be willing to do just about anything to please her. As long as she didn't decide she wanted Wil.

"What's the matter?" she asked, her voice almost a low purr. She dropped her hand to his cock and gave it a gentle squeeze. "I can feel that you're turned on. Uncomfortable?"

What man wouldn't be when his woman confessed to wanting his friend? "A little."

"Poor baby." Her fingers stroked his cock through the thick material of his jeans.

"About Wil—" he started, but she cut his words off with a quick, hot kiss that didn't last nearly long enough.

"You're hard as a rock. Want me to do something about it?" Just the deep tone of her voice was enough to make him feel ready to lose control.

Shit. "Yeah," he said thickly, almost unable to form words.

She smiled sensually as he heard the rasp of his zipper. When she'd freed his cock from the way-too-tight confines of his jeans, her eyes widened. "My, my. I guess you really did enjoy this conversation."

She had no idea. Absolutely *none*. He was about to answer when she dropped to her knees before him and he lost all ability to think. She wrapped her incredible warm, full lips around the head of his cock and sucked him deep into her mouth. He groaned in agony when she pulled away and scooted back along the floor.

"You really need to lay down for this, Royce. I have a lot more freedom to move if I've got you flat on your back."

At that point, he'd give her whatever she wanted as long as she didn't stop. Not for a long, long time. He started to lie back on the couch, but she shook her head. "No. The rug."

He moved to the floor, his whole body shaking, and sprawled on his back on the plush carpet. Merida straddled him, her back to him, her firm, round ass inches from his face. When she took his cock in her mouth again, she took him deep. He felt himself bump up against the back of her throat and groaned. At this rate, she'd kill him in seconds. As her head bobbed up and down on his cock, her ass wiggled in his face. He couldn't take another second without touching.

He gripped her hips and pulled her toward him, bringing her fabric-covered mound to his face. He pressed his nose to her and drew a deep breath, inhaling her musky scent. He tugged at the back pockets of her pants. "Get these off."

She released him long enough to say one word. "Patience."

"I'm not very good with patience." He nipped her ass through her pants as his fingers pressed against her mound. Her breathing hitched. "I want to make it good for you, too, honey. Just take off your pants and I promise I'll make you scream." *Do it soon*, he added silently, getting closer to coming by the second.

She slipped his cock out of her mouth and stood up before him, stripping off her pants and panties far too slowly. She turned and bent over to set them on the floor, giving him a glimpse of her glistening pink pussy. He licked his lips. He couldn't wait to sink his teeth into all that soft skin. "Get back here, Merida. Now."

She climbed back on top of him, leaning over and blowing a hot breath across his cock. "Happy now?"

"I will be when you wrap your pretty lips around my cock again."

She smiled at him over her shoulder. "With pleasure." When she took him back into the hot, wet recesses of her mouth, he pulled her to him and licked his tongue along her slit. She shivered visibly and increased her pace on his cock.

He circled her clit with his tongue, amazed at how wet she'd become. Every stroke of his tongue dragged another muffled moan from her lips. Did the position turn her on this much, or had it been the conversation? If thinking about two men at once did this to her, they might have to revisit that conversation later, when the whole mess with the *Aparasei* had cleared up.

He felt her body bow in orgasm seconds before she shuddered over him. He thrust his tongue inside her just as her cunt gushed her juices. He greedily lapped them up, as his own climax washed over him. He dropped his head back as he came, shouting out her name into the otherwise silent room.

She was absolutely amazing, and he'd be damned if he was going to let her go.

She rolled off him and tried to move away, but he wouldn't let her. He pulled her to him and cuddled her into his side, sliding his hand under her tank top to cup her bare breast. She fought the closeness at first, but soon settled against him, her hand tentatively brushing over his chest.

"That was amazing," he told her truthfully, trying to keep his emotions out of his voice. The thought of anything more than sex with him seemed to make her squeamish. He'd have to move into more permanent territory slowly or risk scaring her away.

"Yeah," she agreed softly, breathlessly. He liked her breathless. That's where she belonged — next to him in bed, naked and breathless. He laughed softly at the thought of trying to explain that to her.

She glanced up at him, her eyes narrowed. "What's so funny?"

"This. Us. Who would have thought that we'd end up like this?"

"Like what? Fucking? Please. I could have told you that would happen the first day we met."

"I'm not talking about the sex." Though it definitely had its benefits. "I mean everything else."

She stilled, her breathing ragged. "There is nothing else."

He let out a deep sigh, reminding himself yet again not to push it. She needed time. He just hoped he had enough time to convince her before she ran away again. With a shake of his head, he changed the subject. "Can I ask you a question?"

"You can ask. I can't guarantee that I'll answer."

He smiled. Typical. "That's fine. You demons don't marry, right?"

"We mate, but don't marry. Marriage is too religious."

That was pretty much what he'd figured after conversations with Ellie about her relationship with Eric. "So why is it, then, that you haven't mated yet?"

"How do you know I haven't?"

Because he'd asked her brother the last time they'd

spoken. Not that he'd ever be stupid to admit that to Merida—especially not with his cock hanging out of his pants. He didn't relish the idea of losing such an important body part. "A good guess?"

"I never found the right man." She paused and drew a deep, shuddering breath. "To be honest with you, I haven't really been looking. I used to, when I was younger, but searching for a *Panthicenos* who fit me perfectly quickly got boring."

"Who says your mate has to be *Panthicenos*?"

She shrugged, her shoulder rising against his side. "It's just the way things are."

"What about Eric? He and Ellie are mated, and she was human when they met."

"But she's not now. She's *Panthicenos*, like Eric."

Interesting. "What if you could have someone who'd truly be your equal? Someone who treated you like the independent woman you are and not some little girl who can't take care of herself? Someone who would love you with all his heart and soul, but not try to stifle you."

She snorted. "If that person existed, I'd be all over him in a second."

She was.

He let out a pained laugh. He might be overprotective at times, but he'd never try to change her. Not in a million years. His life had gotten so much more interesting with her in it.

"Can I ask you a question now?" she asked.

"Yeah. Ask whatever you want."

She lifted her head off his chest and rolled to her side, propping herself up on her elbow. "You said your wife killed herself, right?"

He nodded.

"Is that why you became a vampire?"

He considered lying just to save himself from the emotional drain the story would cause, but Merida deserved better than that. He needed to tell her everything, so there were no secrets between them.

"No. Sarah ran off with my brother, Marco. We all thought he'd died, but he hadn't. He'd been turned. He'd wanted Sarah, and he'd done all he could to get her. She begged him to turn her, and he did."

Royce drew a deep breath and willed himself to continue. He'd never shared the full story with another being, not even Wil. He shuddered as he spoke. "She didn't handle it. Some people just don't. Her body couldn't take the change. It shut down. Slowly. I've heard it's a painful process, organs slowly failing, muscles cramping. It must have been horrible for her. I'd found a vampire and begged him to turn me so I could try to win Sarah back. But by the time I'd found her, it had been too late. She'd taken her own life."

Merida cupped his jaw in her palm, her eyes filled with sadness. "I'm so sorry. Wil turned you, didn't he?" she asked, surprising him.

"Yes. How did you know that?"

She shrugged. "I don't know. I just had a feeling."

"Yeah, he turned me. Things were a lot different for vampires then. There weren't so many laws, no modern police. Wil fed my anger, and I let him. I went a little nuts after Sarah died. I hated her, I hated Marco. I hated the world. But most of all, I hated myself. I must not have been the best husband if she felt the need to leave. I wish I could remember more about that time of my life, but as time passes the memories fade." He laughed bitterly. "The time after she died, though—I don't want to remember any of that."

Times hadn't been the best, and he'd done some things that ashamed him. If he laid it all out, told her his story and she still accepted him, he'd know the possibility of a future between them still existed.

She came back to him and rested her chin on his chest, her arms coming around his sides. "Whatever you have to say, say it. I'll understand."

"I took it out my anger on anything and everything I could get my hands on." He kissed the top of her head, then lifted her chin with his thumb and brushed a kiss across her lips. "I did a lot of things I'm not proud of. Things changed for a little while when I went to work for Sam, but then the old life sucked me right back in. I was a mess, and Sam didn't want me hanging around in that condition."

"I thought you left on your own because you couldn't handle the killing aspect of the job."

He snorted. "Yeah, right. Is that what he told you?" He softened his tone, not wanting to upset her. She was strong, but everyone had their limits. "Trust me, Merida. I had no problem with the killing aspect. What I had a problem with was deciding who my real friends were. Wil had been there for me in the beginning, even though he wasn't the best influence on me at the time, and I felt a lot of loyalty to him."

He felt her stiffen against him. "You chose Wil over Sam. Over the rest of us."

"It's not like that. Sam wanted me to leave. He wanted

me away from you, Merida."

She tilted her head to the side. "I thought you said you didn't even remember me when we met again."

"I barely did. I didn't think much in those days. My mind had shut down. I had to get away from everything for a while, get my head on straight. It took some time, but I eventually got my act together. Got back into healing. Eventually I did the whole medical school thing. I guess it just took me a little longer than most to sow my wild oats."

"You don't seem like that now. I could never see you being nasty."

"Like I said, it was another lifetime ago. I'm sure you understand."

"Better than most."

He shifted under her in discomfort. When she stared down at him, it felt like she could see right into his soul. "I've never told anyone any of that."

"Why did you choose to tell me?"

"Because I knew you, of all people, wouldn't judge me for it. That's what I like about you. You're so caring and understanding. Very maternal." He felt the need to lighten the mood before things got too heavy.

She pinched his side. "Yeah, that's me. I'm a regular mother hen."

She'd be surprised, but sometimes that was exactly how he saw her. She cared more than she would admit to anyone. And maybe she didn't even realize it herself. "I'm sorry," he told her softly.

She frowned at him, her eyebrows drawing together. "For what?"

"Being a royal pain in the ass since we met up again."

"Do me a favor. Don't stop."

That was a surprise. "Why?"

"I kind of like you just the way you are. I like a challenge."

"Believe me, sweetheart, I'm no challenge as far as you're concerned." He brought her hand to his mouth and brushed a kiss over her knuckles.

"Oh, but you are. We clash sometimes."

He had to laugh at that one. "But we make up well."

"We never used to. You couldn't stand me."

"Are you sure? I told you I barely even remember you."

"But I remember you." She tucked her head back against his shoulder, he suspected to hide her eyes deliberately from him.

"What is it that you're not telling me?"

"I had a huge crush on you. Way back then, like three hundred and fifty years ago or something."

His heart hitched in anticipation and his breath caught in his throat. "What about now?"

"Now? Oh, it's more than a crush." She punctuated her semi-playful words with little pokes of her fingernails into his sides.

"How much more?" he winced as she got him between a couple of ribs.

"No classifications, remember? We're just going to go with the flow."

He flung his head back and groaned. He should have known his words would come back to haunt him. "Yeah, I remember. But what happens if I change my mind? What if I want to classify this…thing as something?"

She shrugged, but he could feel the tension slipping from her. "Too bad."

They'd see about that. He'd do whatever it took to convince her otherwise.

"Merida?"

She didn't answer. He listened to her low, deep breathing and glanced down. She was fast asleep. He pulled away from her and stood, picking up her pants and panties before he lifted her off the floor and carried her toward his bedroom. They still needed to discuss the *Aparasei* and what to do about it, but after the conversation they'd had he felt a little drained himself. Daylight would come before he knew it. It might not hurt to get a few extra hours of sleep.

* * * * *

Merida sat at the kitchen table the early next afternoon, a coffee mug clutched in her hands, mulling over the conversation she'd had with Royce last night. Or had it been early this morning? With the irregular sleeping patterns around here, she couldn't keep anything straight. She took a long sip of the steaming drink, her mind stuck on Royce and all he'd told her. He'd opened up, been completely honest about things she'd been surprised to hear him say. But he was right. She wouldn't judge him for what he'd done. If he said he'd changed, she believed it. Living for hundreds of years usually turned out to be like living several lifetimes.

She set the mug down on the tabletop and ran a hand through her hair, trying to untangle some of the curls, still damp from her recent shower. She hadn't been awake long—only an hour or so—and already she wanted to go back to bed. With Royce. When she'd woken up in his bed this morning, with his arms wrapped protectively around her, her first instinct was to bolt. But she stayed, letting herself work through the fear, and finally settled back against him with a tentative sense of tranquility. Because of their open conversation, she felt more at ease with him than she ever had. Now he seemed like a real person to her and not just another man out to show her he was stronger or better than she was. He didn't do that to her. At least not often. She loved that about him. She needed…

Damn it. She didn't *need* the guy.

But she wanted him. More than she'd ever imagine. And for more than just sex—though that did play a pretty big part in her decision. She loved the sex, but it helped a lot that she loved the man, too.

What she'd said to him about Wil…she hoped he knew she'd been kidding. She'd seen the jealousy in his eyes and didn't want to come between a friendship so lasting. She'd only wanted to turn him on. Maybe she'd gone a little too far. She laughed weakly and shook her head, bringing the mug to her lips again. All the sex must be getting to her, turning her brain to mush. Sex, love, and annoyingly perfect—or perfectly annoying—vampires had to wait.

The main problem here, the *Aparasei*, needed to be dealt with first. Soon, before someone else got hurt. She should have figured something out last night, but after finding the message written on the wall she hadn't been in the right state of mind. She should have insisted she and Royce discuss ways to get rid of the evil being, but he'd offered her a distraction and she'd been weak enough to take it. Not for the first time, she questioned Sam's decision to let her stay on the job for so long when she was so obviously incompetent.

She stood up and put her half-full mug in the sink, her appetite for caffeine gone. When she turned, Wil stood in the kitchen doorway, his expression flat. He blinked at her and shook his head. "We're too late."

"What happened?"

He stumbled into the kitchen and pulled out a chair, dropping into it. He let out a rough sigh. "Michelle is dead."

"*What?*" Her heart stopped, her stomach lurching to her throat. "What happened?"

He swallowed convulsively. "A friend of hers found her on her living room floor. She went over this morning when Michelle didn't show up for work. She died sometime last night."

A chill ran through her. Michelle might have been lying there dead when they were right next door. "How did she die?"

"I don't know. The only thing he told me is that they're looking at it as a homicide. The chief won't give me details."

"Why not?"

The hair on the back of her neck rose at the feral look in his eyes. "Probably because I'm a suspect."

Merida pulled out another chair and sat down, facing him across the table. He refused to meet her eyes. "That makes no sense. You were at work last night. You have a solid alibi."

He shook his head, his intense gaze snagging hers and

holding. "I didn't go back to work last night. After you and Royce left, I didn't go back."

She gulped. This didn't sound very good. "What did you do?"

"I didn't hurt Michelle, if that's what you mean. I would never hurt her. I sat in the car, watching her house and trying to debate a few things."

"Like what?" Murder, maybe?

"Like leaving town. Starting over again. I've been here too long anyway." He ran a hand through his dark hair, his eyes never leaving hers. "If I'd seen the problems with her sooner, I might have been able to save her. She had her issues, but she didn't deserve to die."

"It's not your fault. You can't blame yourself." She wanted to scold him for being so stupid about Michelle in the first place, but she couldn't bring herself to do it. He must be going through hell, and as dumb as she thought he'd been to the whole situation, she couldn't add to his pain by pointing it out.

"She was the wrong person to get involved with," he told her, shaking his head. "Maybe if I'd just told her no the first time she'd asked me out, she wouldn't be dead now."

Merida placed her hand over his. "That's not true. This has nothing to do with you. The *Aparasei* killed her. It's too much of a coincidence that the other murders took place just next door." She frowned. She'd assumed the woman Calusius referred to in her dream was Michelle. But he hadn't taken Michelle. He may have killed her instead.

Wil pulled out of her grasp and slowly got up from the chair, looking tired and pained. "I've got to go down to the police station. The chief has a couple of *questions* for me."

"You work for him. He knows what kind of a man you are. Why would he even suspect you're capable of this?"

He shrugged. "People talk. I'm not exactly Mr. Popularity around here. Have you seen my keys?"

"It's the middle of the afternoon. You can't drive. You won't be able to handle the sun for that long. You'll get into an accident."

"Royce is going to drive me in. I already asked him. He's upstairs getting changed."

Not if he wanted to come back in one piece. "Bullshit. Neither one of you is going to endanger your lives. I can handle the sun just fine. I'll drive. You can both sit in back and sleep for all I care."

Wil blinked at her, his gaze uncertain, as if he wasn't used to people being nice to him. "You don't have to do that."

"Actually, if you insist on going somewhere at this time of day, I think I do."

Royce walked into the room then, before she could tell Wil to stop being such an arrogant jerk and accept a little help, and handed her his car keys. "I'd greatly appreciate you driving. We *both* would."

Wil threw his hands in the air in defeat before rustling through a pile of mail on the counter. He finally located his key ring and stuffed it into his pocket. "Okay. Fine. I'm ready to go. Just drive carefully, okay?"

Knowing he must be upset over Michelle's death, she decided not to give him a hard time. She followed Royce and Wil out the front door.

Ten minutes later, they pulled up in front of the small brick building that housed the Caswell PD. "Wait here," Wil said as he climbed out of the back seat and walked toward the glass door. His shoulders hunched as he pulled the door open and disappeared inside.

Royce, sitting beside her in the passenger seat, put his hand on Merida's knee. "What do you think of all this?"

She sighed and shook her head. "I think your friend could be in some pretty big trouble."

"How do you figure?"

"He and Michelle had dated, then had a spat where he says he threatened her—who knows who she might have told about that, and exactly what she said. He didn't go back to work last night, but he didn't check in with anyone, either, so he has no alibi. And you know as well as I do, in a situation like this, a husband or lover is usually pretty high on the suspect list. You know they're never going to find the real killer for any of the recent murders. Wil would be convenient to blame."

He shifted in the car seat. "I didn't think of all that. If they suspect him, I don't know what he's planning to do."

"Trust me, he'll be a suspect. Men are more prone to violent tendencies. At least, that's what the so-called studies lead us to believe." She knew differently, but she also knew there was a big difference between human women and women of other...races. She'd run across a few females who would make an ordinary human male's blood curdle.

"Yeah, so they say." He leaned back even further and closed his eyes. "I hope he has a plan to get out of here fast, or else there could be some serious complications."

Merida nodded. She understood completely. If Wil

was arrested, he wouldn't be able to feed. That would either kill him, or drive him insane.

Wil walked out of the station a few minutes later, a scowl on his face. He pulled his sunglasses out of his shirt pocket and put them on as he walked to the car and slid into the back seat. "Let's go. I need to get out of here."

Royce turned around to face Wil. "What happened?"

"*What happened?* What do you *think* happened?" He leaned back in the seat and turned toward the window. "We'll talk about it later. Now I just want to sleep."

He closed his eyes and stayed silent for the ten minute ride back to his house, but Merida had a feeling sleep was the furthest thing from his mind. He didn't open his eyes until she'd pulled Royce's car into the driveway and switched off the ignition.

When they got inside the house, Wil headed for the stairs without a word to Merida or Royce. She grabbed his arm to stop him from leaving the room.

"What?" He tried to brush her hand away. "It's over now. You should be happy."

"It isn't over. Not even close."

He just snorted and brushed past her into the living room. Royce tried to hold her back, but she ducked out of his grasp and followed Wil.

Royce walked past her, shooting her a warning glare, before stopping in front of Wil. "Do you want to talk about it?"

"There's nothing to talk about." He drew a deep breath and let it out slowly. "Michelle is dead. At this point, I'm pretty high on the suspect list—for as the chief called it, suspicious behavior. I quit, turned in my formal resignation today, so now's a good a time as any to get the hell out of here."

Royce shook his head. "You can't leave yet. This isn't over, no matter what you might think."

"My part in it is." The look in his eyes told a completely different story.

Merida walked up next to Royce, her hands on her hips. If he thought to call Royce here for help and then leave them stranded, he had another think coming. "Yeah, sure. I don't think you're the type to give up in the middle of an investigation."

"You have no idea what type I am. You don't know anything about me."

"I know enough." She tried to sound calm and soothing, but could barely manage it through the stress and anger. "Look, I know you're going through a lot right now, but you need to get over it. You called Royce and me for something, and that hasn't been accomplished yet. We need to work together to take care of Calusius before he tears down the whole town. He told me he wants to take me back with him, and I've got to tell you I'm not giving up without a fight."

Wil's shoulders drooped and he leaned back against the wall. "I honestly don't care what happens."

"Then do it for Michelle. She got mixed up in something she couldn't control. Help me get this guy, and you can get him back for what he did to her. I promise."

He glanced at her, anger filling his heated expression. "Yeah, okay."

She smiled.

"I'll stay and we'll take care of this, but after that I'm gone."

She didn't blame him. Sometimes too much change happened too quickly, and a person had to move on. "What can I do to help you through this?"

Wil mumbled something unintelligible and walked out of the room.

"I'll talk to him. You, stay here." Royce shook his head and started after Wil. "I know you're trying, but you're really not helping."

Huh. She flopped down on the couch and rested her head in her hands. Could this get any worse?

Yes. Of course it could. As much as she liked to think she could handle things on her own, she knew better than to believe that. She took her cell phone out of her purse and dialed Sam's number. He'd know what to do. He always did.

She listened to the phone ring six times before his voicemail picked up. "You've reached Sam Kincaid. Leave a message."

"Nothing like getting right to the point, Sam," she mumbled, waiting for the tone. "Hey, Sam. I need you to call me as soon as you get in. It's really, really important. Crucial. Vital. I need help."

She hit the end button and tapped the phone against her forehead. Hopefully he hadn't gone out of town on a job. If so, she might not hear from him for days.

Chapter Fourteen

Merida stood in the kitchen window, watching Wil pace the backyard. The sun had set an hour ago and he'd been out there ever since, walking aimlessly, staring out into space. He hadn't gone to bed at all since getting the phone call about Michelle, and that worried her. He'd come back downstairs a few minutes after she'd called Sam, dropped onto the couch and turned the TV on. He spent the whole day staring blankly at the screen.

"Is he still out there?" Royce asked as he stepped up next to her and parted the curtains further to look out into the yard.

"Yeah." She let the curtain drop and slid onto one of the stools at the counter bar. "Do you think he's going to be okay?"

Royce alarmed her further by shrugging. "I have no idea. But if he doesn't snap out of this funk soon, he's going to do a lot of harm to himself. Don't say anything, but with all the stress of the last week or so, he hasn't been feeding regularly. Coupled with the fact that he didn't sleep all day...I just don't want to see him hurt himself."

"What can we do to help?"

A cough drew her attention to the back door, where Wil stood leaning against the doorframe. "There's nothing you can do."

She shook her head. "There's got to be something. You need a decent meal and a long rest, and then you'll be as good as new."

"Yeah, right." He pulled out the stool next to her and sat down, leaning his arms on the counter. "It's easy for you to say, since you're not about to be accused of murder."

Royce propped his hip on the counter and crossed his arms over his chest. "No one's accusing you of anything."

"No. Not yet. But I've worked for the police department long enough to know how it works." Wil closed his eyes for a few seconds. When he opened them, he didn't even try to hide the raw pain in his gaze. "There aren't any other suspects, and I don't have an alibi."

Not knowing how to respond, Merida looked over to Royce. He just shook his head. "When's the last time you fed?" he asked his friend.

Wil shrugged without looking up from the countertop. "It's been a while. I don't know. I haven't been keeping track."

"You do know. How long has it been, Wil? You look like shit."

Wil barked a laugh, this time glancing in Royce's direction. "You aren't exactly a beauty queen, Cardoso." He paused and drew a deep breath, letting it out slowly. "It's been a couple of days. Nothing I can't handle."

"Bullshit. You haven't been handling things at all for the last couple of days. You want me to go out with you? We can find some—"

Wil pushed away from the counter, shoving the stool back so hard that it toppled and hit the floor with a crash. "I haven't needed a parent in centuries, and I certainly don't need one now. Mind your own fucking business."

Merida glanced at him. He didn't look fine. He looked

like hell—or worse. "I'm here," she blurted, earning herself a sharp look from Royce. "I can help, if you need me to."

Wil turned to look at her slowly, his dark eyes assessing. "What can you do for me?" he asked, his tone hinting at suspicion.

"You can feed from me."

Hope sparked in his eyes, but then he shook his head. "I couldn't do that to you."

Men. Why did they have to be so pigheaded and stubborn? "At this point, I don't think you have the right to be picky. You never should have let yourself go this long. You have to take what you can get before you're too weak to feed on your own."

He started to protest as Royce stepped around the counter and took Merida's arm in his hands. He brought her wrist to his mouth, the familiar rush of pleasure and pain running through her as his fangs pierced the skin. She let out a small gasp, her gaze locked with Wil's as Royce gently suckled her wrist. Wil licked his lips, his eyes darkening and the muscles of his jaw working. Merida's stomach did a flip-flop as his eyes fell to where Royce's mouth joined her skin. She tried to tamp down a stirring of arousal that curled inside her, but it wasn't easy.

Royce lifted his lips and a drop of blood welled in the wound. She heard Wil's sharp intake of breath followed by a low groan. She knew from experience that a vampire who hadn't fed in a while could become out of control very quickly. The thought scared her and aroused her at the same time.

She shot a quick glance in Royce's direction. What did he have planned?

"Drink, Wil," he said softly, moving her wrist in Wil's direction. Wil held back for all of two seconds before he clamped his mouth over her waiting flesh. He sucked hard, a sharp pain running up the inside of her arm—the effects of a starving, grieving man. She expected anger, maybe jealousy from Royce, yet if he felt the emotions, they didn't show in his eyes. He looked at her like he wanted to eat her alive. *Oh, God.* Her mouth went dry and her pulse kicked in double-time.

"Are you okay with this?" he asked her. She nodded, getting the feeling he was talking about more than Wil's feeding.

"Let me know if you aren't, okay?"

"I'm fine. Really." She was better than fine. It was almost too much to take.

And then Royce moved behind her, his hands moving aside her hair, his lips on the skin where her shoulder joined her neck. When she felt his fangs bite into her, she nearly came. A spasm ran through her cunt and she gasped for air. Before meeting Royce, she hadn't thought of the whole fang and blood-drinking thing as sexy, but this didn't compare to anything in her experience—and all they'd touched her with so far were their teeth.

So far? That nearly pulled her out of her sensual trance. How far did she expect this to go? Did she actually want it to go further than just a group feeding? Did *they*?

Wil swirled his tongue around her wrist before he released her. Her arm flopped down to her side, as limp and useless as the rest of her body. If she hadn't been sitting, she would have pooled on the floor in a big puddle of hormones.

"Thank you," he leaned in and whispered against her

cheek, his hot breath tickling her ear. She whimpered, ready to drag Royce upstairs and tear all his clothes off.

Wil pulled away from her slowly, his lips dragging across her cheek and setting off tiny lines of flame. His gaze locked with hers as he cupped her face in his palm. Her muscles went weak, melted by the heat in his eyes. Moisture pooled in her pussy and she shifted in her seat, the wooden stool growing increasingly more uncomfortable. She expected Wil to walk away, but she should have known better. Nothing in this encounter seemed to go as she'd thought it would.

He leaned in and kissed her.

Wil's lips were firm and warm, full and sensual. She parted her lips in surprise and his tongue snaked into her mouth, swirling with hers. She braced herself for Royce's angry reaction, but he just stayed behind her, his grip on her shoulders tightening. He'd stopped feeding at some point—she couldn't remember exactly when—and he traced the lines of her neck with his mouth. She reached back and dug her hands into his hips, pulling him hard against her. His erection pressed into her back as she wriggled against him.

She felt hands on her breasts, skimming her nipples through her shirt. She almost pulled away, until she realized they were Royce's hands. Was he okay with this, or did he *not* see that Wil's lips kept sucking on hers?

Wil's mouth left hers, his tongue dipping into the hollows of her collarbone. She threaded her hands in his dark hair, the silky smooth texture soft against her palms. She didn't know how long Royce would accept this, or if she should let it continue. All she knew, all she could think about, was that she didn't want it to end anytime soon.

"How are you doing?" Royce asked.

"Um, fine." *For a woman about two seconds away from losing her mind.*

"Stand up," he told her, stepping back to allow her the space to carry out his request. She stood, but had to grip the edge of the counter for support.

She didn't need to worry about falling, though, because almost as soon as she was off the stool Wil pulled her against him, crushing her body to his as he resumed the kiss. Her mind nothing more than a big pile of sensual mush, she wrapped her arms around his neck and gave in. For a few seconds. But then she felt Royce's chest—and other, harder parts of his body—against her back and she pulled away from Wil, shaking and panting.

"I'm fine with this," Royce told her, his mouth against her neck. "If you're okay with it, it won't bother me. If you want us to stop, tell me now."

Was he asking what she thought? "You mean...all of us?"

"Yes," Royce nearly hissed in her ear. "All of us."

"Are you out of your mind?" she asked, but the words lacked conviction. In truth, she'd never been so turned on in her life. What woman wouldn't want two big, gorgeous guys fawning all over her? But she didn't want to mess everything up with Royce, or ruin his friendship with Wil.

"Do you want me to stop?" Wil asked, nibbling tiny kisses down the side of her neck. "I can leave and let you two have some time alone to finish this."

"Don't you *dare*. Not unless you want me to take out your heart with a Popsicle stick," she blurted without thinking.

His laugh, and Royce's, vibrated against her skin,

surrounding her in a cocoon of masculine heat.

"I take it you're enjoying yourself?" Wil asked between tickling kisses.

"Like you can't tell."

He smiled at her, a hint of the man she'd met when they first came to Caswell showing through his mask of despair.

A thought hit her at that moment. They were both a little too comfortable with this situation. They'd eased her into it as if it was the most natural thing in the world. "Is this something the two of you have done together before?"

Both men froze. She couldn't see Royce's face, but he spoke. "We've...shared before. Once or twice," he told her with a teasing edge.

"Oh," she managed before Wil kissed her again, his tongue sliding into her mouth as his hand slid up the inside of her thigh. She cried out in surprise when he cupped her denim-covered mound in his palm. The whole thing still seemed surreal. Was it really happening, or the byproduct of an overactive imagination? No. *Not a dream.* She'd felt the sting of their fangs too sharply for it to be anything but reality. *And what a reality it was.*

"Are you sure this is okay with you?" she asked Royce when Wil broke the kiss. She didn't need him to hate her after this, not when they'd come this far.

He ground his rigid cock against her in answer. "What do you think?"

She had a little trouble in the thinking department, and the more they touched her, the worse it got. "I need to sit back down."

Royce chuckled, and it sounded strained. "I think we should lay you down instead."

She couldn't agree more. She didn't remember exactly how it happened, but someone carried her up the stairs into Royce's bedroom. And then Wil was over her, his hands working the hem of her shirt out of her waistband and pulling it over her head. Her jeans and underthings quickly followed, landing in a heap on the plush carpet. She sat on the edge of the bed and Wil knelt down in front of her, parting her knees and wedging his body between them. She ran her hands up his chest and down to the front placket of his pants. He was hard, and hot, and strong. Like Royce. She gulped. Could she handle two men at one time? Sure, it sounded great in theory, but she didn't know if her body could take it without shutting down.

Wil leaned down and captured one of her nipples in his mouth, his fangs scraping against the sensitive flesh. She moaned, her back arching to bring her closer to him. His hands came up her back and held her against him as his tongue laved and his lips teased. He released one nipple and moved on to the other, his touch as drugging as his kiss had been.

Royce came up behind her, pulling her down with him on the bed so she faced him instead of Wil. He pulled her leg over his hip and ground his cock against her. She felt how hard he was even through the layers of his pants and boxers. The rough fabric abraded her sensitive sex, brushing her clit in the most enticing way. Her hands flew to his ass and cupped him, squeezing. He really didn't have any idea how close she was to ripping the things off him.

And Wil's clothes, too. He ran his hand up and down her nude back in teasing strokes, only increasing the fire burning inside her. She needed more. This just wasn't enough. She was just about ready to come out of her skin. She opened her mouth, but all that came out was a strangled moan as Wil kissed his way down her back, he sunk his fangs into the skin of her hip, just above her ass.

She bucked hard against Royce, who appeased some of her need with delicate strokes of his fingers along her pussy. He slid first one, then two fingers inside her, plunging as deep as he could go. She moaned, a long and low keening sound that turned into a growl of pleasure. Her first orgasm took her by surprise, striking like lightning as Royce skimmed his thumb over her clit. She convulsed hard, her vision fading. As she started to come back down someone rolled her to her back and pushed her legs apart. A soft, wet and warm touch feathered over her pussy — a tongue. She snapped her gaze up. Wil's tongue. *Oh God.* There was something illicit yet exciting about Royce watching another man pleasure her.

Wil moved his tongue in slow strokes and swirls over her pussy, never touching where she really needed him. Her flesh still quivered from the first orgasm, but she needed more. A lot more. And soon. Her body was wound tight, ready to snap. Royce's hands covered hers, moving them to Wil's head. She tangled her fingers in Wil's hair, giving him a little push as she raised her hips, silently telling him what she needed. She felt the bed move as Royce stood up. A few seconds later, she heard the rasp of a zipper, sounding unusually loud to her overwhelmed senses. The bed dipped when he rejoined her, laying his naked body next to her as his mouth covered hers and he kissed her deeply. He cupped her breast in his palm and squeezed, his thumb flicking across her nipple. Her hold on Wil's hair tightened as she felt the stirrings of another orgasm build in her belly. Royce's hands were everywhere—or at least that's what it felt like—as her body exploded yet again in another powerful climax. She went limp on the mattress, her eyes closed and her nerves humming in satisfaction.

"Merida," Royce whispered in her ear. "Are you okay?"

She started to nod, but then shook her head. "Can't move. Can't think."

She didn't even protest when he rolled her to her stomach and raised her onto her hands and knees. Her arms threatened to give out and she locked her elbows to keep from falling. "Royce, I can't. I'm done."

"Oh, I don't think so." He parted her folds and rubbed the tips of his fingers along her swollen, sated pussy. "*Mine*," he growled as he slammed his cock into her.

She'd thought she couldn't take any more, but she'd been wrong. Desire heated her blood to a boil as Royce slammed into her, his thrusts harsh and erratic.

Wil stood next to the bed, watching intently. She realized he'd stripped off his clothes at some point—she'd been too involved in the pleasure of it all to notice when. The man had an incredible body. He was leaner than Royce, and a few inches shorter, with well-defined muscles. A detailed tattoo of a dragon graced the skin of his right hipbone, and another—a snake—wrapped around his upper arm. He had his hand wrapped around his very impressive cock and she whimpered at the sight. "Come here, Wil."

"I want to taste," she told him when he hesitated. He groaned and came back to join them on the bed. Royce's hands tightened almost imperceptibly on her hips when Wil knelt in front of her.

She tasted the tip of his cock with her tongue, licking off the drop of precum that had formed there, just before she took his entire length into her mouth. Royce's strokes grew faster, harder, and she had trouble keeping a rhythm with the strokes of her mouth and tongue. Royce's fingers found her clit and pinched down on the sensitive nerves. She felt him tighten behind her just as Wil withdrew from her mouth—and then she came again, and everything ceased to exist except her convulsing body and pounding pulse. Moans filled the room, but she didn't know whose mouths they came from. She didn't care.

She collapsed to the bed, flat on her stomach. Royce came down on top of her, his body half-covering hers, his breathing just as erratic. Wil lay on his back, his eyes narrowed to slits, his gaze focused on the ceiling. Up until she saw his flaccid cock, she didn't even know if he'd come.

She smiled to herself, her eyelids drooping in sated sleepiness. In the morning, she'd probably wonder why she'd let it go that far, but for now she just wanted to savor the hum in her blood.

Royce kissed the back of her shoulder, mumbling something incoherent, and Wil glanced her way and smiled. Regrets? Nah. She might not be willing to let it happen again, but it had definitely been worth it.

* * * * *

Wil woke up a few hours later, tangled in the sheets and the warm woman next to him. He gave her a last look before sliding out of bed. Would she forgive them for what happened a few hours ago?

He hoped so. Royce cared about the woman, more

than he obviously wanted to admit, and Wil would hate to see something like their playtime come between them. Merida cared for Royce, too, but Wil didn't know who he'd call more stubborn. He laughed softly. A match made in heaven if he'd ever seen one. Now if they could both stop being so mulish for a few seconds, they might actually see how perfect they were for each other.

If he didn't screw it all up by staying last night, when he'd known he should have walked away.

He glanced back toward the bed. Royce snuggled closer to Merida, pulling her into his arms. A pang of emptiness hit Wil hard as he remembered all that had happened. Michelle was dead. Last night, Merida had offered him comfort, and he'd greedily taken all he could get. Royce, of course, hadn't minded. They'd shared many times over the years—more than the once or twice they'd told her. Wil had no problems with it, and Royce never had before—but they'd never shared a woman one of them cared about. Tonight they'd moved into new territory.

This would probably be the last time he'd share a woman with Royce. The man was so lost he had no hope of finding his way out. Wil had his standards, low as they might be, and he refused to get in the way of a lasting commitment.

He felt a hand on his shoulder just before he heard Merida speak. "Are you okay?"

He smiled down at her. "Yeah. Fine. Are you?"

She nodded, coming to stand next to him by the railing, her gaze drifting to the backyard. "About last night…"

He had to laugh at the anxiety in her tone. "Listen, if

you're uncomfortable, I'm sorry. That wasn't my intention."

"I'm not uncomfortable with it. It's just something new." She sighed softly, and it made him smile. "Are you going to come back to bed?"

He cupped her chin in his hand and tilted her head up. "Last night was incredible. But it can't happen again."

"Why not?"

"I'm not going to interfere with what you and Royce have."

"We don't—"

He shook his head to stop her false protests. "Yes, you do. Just make sure you notice it before it's too late."

"Are you talking about Michelle?"

He shook his head. The woman his thoughts turned to had died hundreds of years ago. "I'm talking about you and Royce. I've known him forever, and I've never seen him like this. But he's been so closed off for so long reaching out to him isn't going to be easy."

"Who says I want to?"

"You do. With your eyes and with your actions."

He almost laughed at the idea of giving relationship advice to a woman he'd had sex with less than three hours ago.

"I do not," she scoffed, her nose wrinkled. "Do I really?"

He nodded. "Yeah, but it's not just you. He does it, too. I've never seen him act this way over a woman, so you must be pretty special to him."

She snorted. "Yeah. Right. I'm just a warm body— food and sex. That's all."

"You and I both know how untrue that is."

She seemed to mull over his words for a while before she nodded. "Okay. I suppose that's a possibility."

He saw so much more than that in their relationship, but he wasn't in the mood to argue. But if he didn't leave the house for a while, he might end up climbing back into bed with her. Once, Royce would probably forgive. Twice…it seemed doubtful. "Go back to bed with your man. I'm going to go out for a run before the sun comes up."

He leaned in and kissed her gently on the lips before she walked back to bed and snuggled up against Royce. Wil went into his own bedroom and threw on a pair of sweats and an old t-shirt, getting ready to burn off a little more steam. Tonight had helped, but it would be a long time before he'd be able to relax again.

Chapter Fifteen

Merida burrowed under the covers and rested her head on Royce's chest. He was warm, his skin firm and soft, and she loved it. She loved *him*. She'd be glad, though, if he didn't hate her for acting like such a...well, a slut, for lack of a better term. She'd been a wanton hussy, and they'd both gone along with it, provoking her and stroking her, giving her the best orgasms of her life.

She wrinkled her nose. She'd thought she knew everything there was to know about herself, until Royce had come along. He'd shown her things she loved that she'd always thought to be turnoffs. Spanking, tying her up—an evening interlude with his big, hunky friend...she rolled her eyes and began to wonder if she was developing psychological problems.

Aggravated, she poked Royce in the side. He grumbled and blinked his eyes open. "What was that for?" he asked, his voice sleep-husky.

"Nothing special." *For making me fall in love with you, you big jerk. For showing me things you can do to me that ruined all other men for me.*

He smiled slowly, his eyes sharpening a little as he lifted his head from the pillow. "Where's Wil?"

"He went for a run."

Royce's expression grew serious. He rolled to his side, his intense gaze locking with hers. "Are you angry with me about last night?"

"No. It was great."

"It's not going to happen again," he told her, his voice nearing a growl.

She blinked, shocked at his vehemence. "Why not?"

"Because I don't want either of you getting any ideas."

He kissed her, hard and fast, rolling her to her back on the mattress before she could utter a protest.

"I won't. Believe me," she assured him, trying to contain the laughter at his attitude.

He looked down at her, his smile tentative. "Really?"

"Of course. What are you, dumb or something? I only want you. That's the way it's always been." She pinched his hip when he leaned down and nipped her jaw. "Last night took me by surprise. Do me a favor, though. No more surprises like that, okay?"

"Is this that silly childhood crush talking?" he asked, his expression humored.

"Nope. Sorry. This isn't a crush."

"Damned straight." He slid his hands under her naked ass and pulled her closer. When he thrust inside her, it felt right. So right, she almost couldn't help the tear that tried to slip down the side of her cheek.

Royce stopped what he was doing. "What's wrong? Why are you crying?"

"You scare the hell out of me."

He laughed. "Believe me, the feeling is very, very mutual." He stroked inside her, his strokes lengthening and slowing. For the first time, it felt like they made love. It wasn't about just the sex anymore. Now neither of them could deny it. She closed her eyes and grasped his shoulders, her fingers digging into his firm muscles. It was all too much, too soon, and she felt like she might burst from the emotions. She arched her hips, pumping to meet him thrust for thrust, digging her nails into his back as a slow, shimmering orgasm rolled through her body. Royce came soon after, a low groan escaping his lips as he brushed a kiss over her forehead.

He collapsed on top of her, burying his head against the side of her neck. "Wil is going to be back soon."

She let out a long, deep sigh. "Yes, I suppose he is."

"We have some work to do today. I suppose we should get up and get dressed."

"You're right. Give me five minutes."

"I'll get in the shower first."

She watched Royce collect a set of clean clothes and head out of the room. He gave her a smile over his shoulder before he walked out of sight. She didn't move until she heard the shower start a little while later. Then she pulled herself out of bed and dragged her tired body to her room to get her own clothes ready. She pushed a hand through her tangled curls and shook her head. The sun hadn't even come up yet, and already the day seemed ruined. Playtime was over. Now the real work began. Calusius wouldn't even know what hit him.

Her cell phone rang as she pulled a pair of socks from her bag. She snatched it up from the dresser where she'd left it earlier and answered it, relieved when she heard Sam's voice on the line.

"What's up?" he asked. "Your message sounded troubled."

"There's an *Aparasei* here."

Sam whistled long and low. "Shit. You okay?"

She took a deep breath, praying her courage held out. "I don't think so. I don't know what to do to get rid of it."

"Fire, honey. Fire kills them."

Okay, she could do that. No problem. Maybe. "Fire with matches?"

"No. The psychic kind." He paused, his silence conveying a lot more than words would have. "Is there some reason you aren't able to create fire with magic?"

Here we go. "Well, I'm not exactly sure. He marked me. Twice. But that whole thing about being marked and not being able to defeat them is just a legend, right?"

"I'm afraid not," Sam answered in a quiet voice. "It's true. You're going to need somebody else to help you with this."

"Sam? Is there something you're not telling me?"

"I'm leaving in a few minutes. It shouldn't take me more than a couple hours to get there. Give me the address so I can go online and get directions."

"Sam? What's going on?"

His sigh echoed over the phone lines. "Being marked by an *Aparasei* isn't a good thing. We'll talk about it when I get there."

She gave him Wil's address and pressed the end button, sinking down on the mattress. What the hell had he meant by all that? She'd have to wait hours to find out.

* * * * *

She didn't dare tell Royce about her conversation with Sam. Some things were better left a surprise. After his shower he'd gone to bed for a nap—something he'd need since he'd have to face Sam later. After what had happened this week, she didn't imagine it would be a pleasant situation.

An hour had passed since her conversation with Sam, and she'd been on edge the whole time. She needed to find out what Sam had been talking about. And she knew where to go for her information. Wil had come back from his run a little while ago and gone right upstairs to shower. She waited outside the bathroom door.

"We need to talk," she said to him when he swung the door open and stepped into the hall.

He glanced at her nervously before glancing down the hall to the closed door of Royce's room. "I thought we already had that talk."

"Not *that* talk. I'm talking about the *Aparasei*."

He sighed, some of the tension draining from his shoulders. "Oh, that. Okay. Fine. Come talk to me while I get dressed."

She gulped. Did she really want to do that? Would it upset Royce? Probably. She quickly followed Wil into his bedroom.

He dropped the towel and she didn't look—really—at his toned ass while he pulled on a pair of boxers. What she did see was something she'd missed last night—the long, thin scars that peppered his back. "Where did you get those scars? Someone really did a number on you."

He stiffened. "Oh, those. I'd forgotten all about them."

"Yeah, sure you did." She looked closer at the scars, which resembled the one on her arm. "Those are from an *Aparasei*, aren't they?"

He sighed as he stepped into a pair of black jeans. Once he zipped them, he sat on the edge of the bed to put on his socks. "I had a little run-in with one a few years back. It's nothing."

"What do you mean nothing? He hit me once and knocked me out cold. You look like you took at least twelve blows with whatever magic they use." She couldn't keep the suspicion out of her tone. What was he hiding from her?

"Fifteen," he said softly, his gaze drifting to anything but her. He stood up and pulled a red t-shirt over his head, tucking it into the waistband of his jeans.

She winced at just the thought. "What happened?" she asked quietly.

"My epiphany." He laughed bitterly as he ran a hand through his hair. "I was a little...um, wild quite a few years ago. I got tangled up in some things better left alone, and got attacked by an *Aparasei*. I probably should have been dead—wished I was for a couple of days—but I survived. They only kill when they want to, but they're able to inflict a good deal of pain."

She ran the tip of her finger down his shirt over one of the scars she remembered seeing. It started just below his right shoulder and trailed all the way down to his left hip. "Ouch."

He flinched away from her touch. "Yeah."

"Wil?"

He turned to her, his eyebrow raised, as he threaded a black leather belt through his belt loops.

"Have you ever been married?"

"A long time ago. Another lifetime."

"That's pretty much what Royce said when I asked him about Sarah."

He finally smiled. "Yeah, this life bites sometimes.

You can never hold on to anything long enough."

"What happened to your wife?"

"Elizabeth died. In childbirth, of all things." He shook his head. "She wasn't ready to turn for me. She told me to give it a few years, she still had some living she wanted to do. Turns out she would have been safer as a vampire than she was as a human."

Merida blinked, almost afraid to ask her next question. "What happened to the baby?"

"Stillborn." Wil shook his head, his expression pained. "I should have realized that would happen."

"Wait a second. You mean she was human, and you...you got her pregnant?"

He nodded. "An accident. I wanted to wait until she'd turned vampire and could carry the baby safely."

"I didn't think that was possible."

"Believe me, Merida, it's entirely possible." He sat down once again on the side of the bed, his eyes bleak and tired. "As I said, though, that was another lifetime ago. I've done my best to forget it, okay?"

She took that as her cue to leave the room or change the subject. "I called Sam Kincaid, my former boss."

"You did?" Wil looked surprised. "From what Royce has told me, I thought the two of you didn't get along."

"We'll have to. He's coming to help." She shook her head. "He confirmed what you said about being marked. I can't do anything to get rid of him, and Royce doesn't have the capability. So, I think Sam is our only option at this point."

"You're probably right. When will he be here?"

"In an hour or two."

Wil walked to his closet and pulled out a huge, navy blue suitcase. He set it on the bed, unzipped it, and started emptying his dresser drawers into it.

"What are you doing?" Merida asked as he scooped a stack of t-shirts from a drawer and stuffed them into the suitcase.

"Getting ready." He paused what he was doing long enough to frown at her. "Maybe you should pack your own things while you wait for your boss. I don't think it's such a good idea to come back here after Sam gets rid of this thing."

"Okay." She started to walk out of the room, but turned back to him. "If you ever want to talk, I'm willing to listen."

He glanced at her and smiled before returning to his packing. "Thanks."

"You'll keep in touch, right? Let me know how you're doing?"

His gaze locked with hers and she saw the sincerity in his eyes. "Of course. I never forget my friends. I don't keep many of them, so I make sure to stay in touch with the ones important to me."

She left the room to pack her things, a genuine smile on her face for the first time in what seemed like ages.

* * * * *

When Sam pulled his car into Wil's driveway, Merida let out a breath of relief. She stood on the front porch, her arms crossed over each other to ward off the chill of the dreary day. Her relief lasted until the second Sam got out of the car and slammed the door, fixing her with an icy glare.

"What the hell have you been doing?" he asked as he climbed the porch steps. "Why can't you just stay out of trouble? The whole ride here, I've been worried sick."

"Bullshit. You never worry about me."

He raised an eyebrow at her, his gaze furious. "Wanna bet? I *do* worry about you. I always have. You're like a daughter to me. I worry about you even when you take off for months at a time without even bothering to call me and let me know you're okay. I don't want to see anything happen to you."

Taken aback by his emotional confession, she shook her head. "Then why did you let me work for you, doing such dangerous work?"

"I know you. If I didn't let you, you would do it on your own. At least if you work for me, I can keep an eye on you." He shook his head and laughed. "Your brother wants you to call him — in his words, so he can verbally kick your ass for getting close enough to an *Aparasei* to let it touch you."

She frowned and hugged her arms tighter around her body. "I had a good reason to."

"I'm sure you did. That doesn't change what happened."

"And what, exactly is that? You told me we'd talk about it when you got here. You're here. Start talking."

"Inside," he told her. She swung the door open and Sam followed her into the house.

"Where's Cardoso? Sleeping, I assume?"

"He's packing. He and Wil will be down in a few minutes." She didn't tell Sam that she'd asked them to give her a few minutes alone with Sam before the real work started. She wanted to find out what problems the mark had caused her, and she didn't want Royce in the room to hear what Sam had to say.

"Why, if you knew there was a huge problem going on here, did you not call for help sooner?" Sam asked.

"I didn't realize it was this big. I thought Royce and I could handle it."

Sam looked around the room before his gaze came back to her. "I don't think it's a good idea for you to spend too much time with the vampire."

"Why?"

"Vampires are unpredictable. *Panthicenos* are not. We are by nature careful and methodical... Well, at least most of us are," he added with a meaningful glance at her. "The two of you aren't a good match."

She fought the urge to yell and scream—exactly what he wanted her to do, to make his point for him. Instead, she bit back her snappish reply. "Point duly noted. So what's going to be our best course of action here?"

Sam said nothing, but she knew from his expression that she'd made him curious with her behavior. She used that to her advantage when she asked her next question. "What's going to happen to me now that I've been marked?"

Sam surprised her—and worried her—by pulling her into a hug. "I've been worried about you this past year," he told her before he let her go.

"What's wrong with me? Am I going to die or something?" she asked him, her eyes wide.

Sam stared at her for a long time before he finally spoke. "No. You're not going to die. You won't be able to serve as a Balance Keeper, either, though."

She knew she shouldn't be happy about that, but she couldn't help the smile that came to her face. "Why not?"

"The High Council that governs the Balance Keepers sticks pretty rigidly to the old traditions. It used to be believed that being marked by a purely evil being tainted one's blood, making them evil. We know differently now, at least most of us do. But the High Council is still stuck in the dark ages. Any being marked by evil is not allowed to serve the Council in any purpose. But, I'm sure you're perfectly fine with this new twist."

"Oh, I'm devastated."

He actually laughed. "You know you can come back to work for me any time, right? My business isn't governed by the High Council."

"No thanks. I'm going to take more time to sit back and enjoy life. I've liked my freedom a little too much."

Sam nodded, his friendly expression shifting back to the professional one. "I think you should pack up and go home. Take Cardoso with you. I'll take care of it from here."

"No. Not again. You are not going to take this away from me. It's my job. *Mine.* I got here first. Don't make me sorry I called you for help."

"I don't mean to upset you, honey, but you haven't exactly had the best history for doing as told, or getting rid of demons."

"I got rid of Aiala."

"After I specifically asked you not to try."

"To avoid an argument, I'm going to go and see what's keeping Royce and Wil. I'll be back in a few minutes." She turned and rushed out of the room before she said a whole bunch of things she'd later regret.

When she knocked on Royce's door, it swung open. She stepped inside the room to see him lying flat on his back on the mattress, snoring softly. "Of all the times to take a nap."

She walked over to the bed and kicked his shin. No response. She leaned close to his ear. "Hey Royce?"

Still nothing. She blew out a sharp breath and sunk her teeth into the side of his neck, figuring a little biting would be a good way to wake up a vampire.

Bad idea. Before she could even back away, he had her pinned to the mattress beneath her. "What the fuck was that all about?"

She drew a shaky breath. "Sorry. I didn't think you'd react so strongly."

"Well, I did. Now you've got to deal with it." He leaned in and kissed her hard, but she pushed him away.

"Not now, Royce. We've got to talk."

He rolled off her with a groan. "What is it?"

"Sam is here. He's insisting on taking over."

Royce's expression darkened, his eyes the color of thunderclouds. "What the hell is he doing here?"

"I kind of called him." She jumped off the bed and walked toward the door. "Meet me downstairs in five, okay?"

"Stop right there." He pointed a finger at her, his eyes narrowed. "You *kind of* called him? Either you did, or you didn't."

"Okay, I did, but I only thought he'd come in here to help. I didn't think he'd take over and send me home."

Royce sighed and shook his head. "Shit. Any suggestions, genius? You're the one who brought him into this. I wish you'd talked to me about it first."

"Sorry. I didn't know this would happen."

"How could you not? You know what kind of a man Sam is."

"I know he helped Eric raise me. He's the closest thing to a father I have."

Royce laughed humorlessly. "Then I won't upset you by telling you what a ruthless bastard the guy really is. I guess you wouldn't want to know that."

She snorted. "Shut up. He's not as bad as you think."

"And he's not as good as you seem to think, either."

She'd give him that. She'd seen Sam at work, and she knew Royce spoke the truth. Still, she didn't like anyone insulting her family. "Okay. We can disagree on this later. Right now, we have an *Aparasei* to stop—who can only be destroyed by psychic fire, by the way, which I can't use on him since I've been marked. Sam can do it, so I think we need to let him stay. I'm staying, too. I want to see this through to the end."

"Me, too." Royce walked over to her and tucked a strand of her hair behind her ear. "Plus, I'm not leaving you until I know you're safe."

Merida's heart thudded to a stop in her chest and she felt a tear well in her eye. He planned to leave her once she was safe? *I wish I'd known that sooner, Big Guy*, she said to herself. *I never would have let myself fall in love with you.*

She batted the tear away as she left the room. She'd known to expect it. She'd survive, somehow. She always did.

* * * * *

Sam pulled his car to a stop in front of the house where they hoped to find Calusius, and Merida climbed out of the passenger seat. She'd been fighting hard to keep the tears at bay since her conversation with Royce, and so far she'd done okay. When Sam had asked her what was wrong, she'd told him Calusius's promise to take her back with him upset her. Sam bought it—or, at least she thought he did. If he doubted her, he didn't tell her.

Royce pulled up behind Sam, with Wil driving up last. He parked across the street and met the rest of them in front of the house. A gray gloom hung in the damp, humid air, appropriate weather for what they were about to do. "I hope you know what you're doing," she said to Sam.

"Of course I do."

She glanced up at him. He didn't look even the least bit nervous. Well, someone out of the bunch of them had to be confident.

Royce came up next to her and took her hand, squeezing gently. The tears she'd been holding back started to flow then, and she tried to pull away. She shook her head when he wouldn't let her go, but he pulled her into a hug and kissed the top of her head. "It'll be okay. I promise."

Anger spiked in her at his tender words. Her tears drying up, she yanked herself out of his grasp. "No shit. Sam knows what he's doing."

"That's not what I meant."

"Save it for someone who gives a damn, vampire." She walked toward the house, not wanting to prolong the inevitable any longer. The sooner they finished this, the sooner she could have Sam drive her to the airport so she could go back home and soak in the sun — and forget about an annoying vampire who said he loved her but didn't really mean it.

Sam brushed past her as soon as she opened the front door. Royce and Wil followed. To her surprise, Calusius stood in the center of the living room, his eyes glowing, waiting for her. "Are you ready, little cat?" He cackled, a sound that made her want to cover her ears.

"Did you kill the woman who lived next door?" Merida asked, stepping further into the room.

"Of course." He made a sweeping gesture with his hand. "I did what I had to do. She belonged to me. Her father promised me his firstborn child years ago, even though he'd planned to have no children. I made sure that the child was conceived. I don't abide by anyone breaking their bargains."

"Why did you kill her?" Wil asked, his hands balled into fists at his side.

"She refused to accept her fate." Calusius glanced at Merida. "You will not be given the opportunity. I see you've brought another cat, my dear. How fun."

"Shut up," she told him, her blood pounding with her anger. Why did he treat this all like some big joke? "You're going to die today."

"Funny," Calusius said softly. "I was going to say the same to you."

He ambled toward her, his gait surprisingly fast given the round, odd shape of his body. When he got a few feet from her, he reached out his hand. Sam waved a hand in the air in his direction and sent him spiraling back against the wall. "The lady is right, *Aparasei*."

Sam raised his hands in the air to shoulder height and made a sweeping motion. Balls of fire burst from his palms, shooting out in all directions. The flames hit the walls, the furniture, and the curtains. Merida blinked as the flames licked up the white walls, charring them black. The curtains disappeared and the fire began to spread across the floor toward them. Soon flames engulfed the far side of the room.

Calusius screamed, a long, high-pitched sound that made Merida's head ache. Royce grabbed her arm and tried to pull her behind him, but she pulled out of his grasp just as Calusius jumped in the air and launched himself toward her. She felt Royce's hand on her arm, heard him call her name, but she could only focus on Calusius moving toward her, as if in slow motion. Just as he came close enough to touch, Sam reached out and grabbed him by the hood of his cloak and threw him back into the flames.

The fire engulfed him, melting his grayed flesh, charring the clothes, turning his glowing eyes to a dull pale gray. He exploded, the ash from his body spraying all over the room—and all over them. Royce cleared his throat, Wil coughed, and Sam grabbed her arm. "We need to get out of here before the flames reach us."

They hurried out the door and stumbled to the front yard just as the entire house burst into flames. They all stood there gaping at the mess, no one saying anything. Merida shook her head, still in shock from how close she'd come to being a part of some evil being's collection.

Royce broke the silence when he turned to Wil. "What are the chances no one in town is going to notice this?"

Wil barked a laugh. "None."

"Then let's get out of here." Royce turned to Merida. "Are you riding with me?"

She shook her head. "I don't think so."

She got into Sam's car without even glancing his way. Sam got behind the wheel a few seconds later and they sped away from the house, following Wil's car through the back roads out of town.

"Are you okay?" Sam asked once they'd left the limits of Caswell.

"I'll survive."

"That isn't what I asked."

She shrugged and leaned back against the soft leather seat. She should feel happy, exhilarated that she'd made it out alive — that they all had — but she couldn't quite muster up the emotion. She felt empty, flat. Deserted by the man she loved with all her heart. The *only* man she'd ever loved. It would be a long time before she recovered from this.

A half hour into the silent drive, Wil pulled his car into the parking lot of a tiny roadside inn. Royce, in between them, followed, with Sam bringing up the rear. "What are we doing?" she asked him. "They're day sleepers. We're not."

"Just give me a few minutes. I want to go inside and see if I can get you a cup of coffee and something to eat. You look like you need it."

Sam got out of the car and followed Royce into the little cottage that served as the motel's office. Merida unbuckled her seatbelt and got out of the car, stretching her arms over her head. She smiled weakly when she saw Wil approach.

"Thanks for everything. I appreciate it."

"Thanks for what? I ruined everyone's lives."

He shook his head and pulled her close for a hug. "Don't even start. It's over. Be happy that you're alive. Where did Sam go?"

"To get us something to eat. I guess this is goodbye."

Wil frowned at her and dropped his arms from around her. "Where are you going? You're not going to go with Royce?"

"I can't. He doesn't want me."

"That's bull and you know it." Wil put his hands on her shoulders and squeezed lightly. "If you leave, it's going to kill him."

"It'll kill me if I stay, only to have him walk away now that he knows I'm safe."

She glanced toward the office and saw Sam start toward the door. "I'd better get back in the car. Sam doesn't like to be kept waiting."

"Merida."

"I've made up my mind. Deal with it."

"Fine. Just take care of yourself, okay." Wil leaned in and kissed her, hard and fast. "Just for the record, Merida, I think you're making a huge mistake."

She shook her head as she got back into the car to wait for Sam. Walking away was the only thing in this whole mess she'd done right.

Chapter Sixteen

She'd walked away from him. Again. And it had damned near torn his heart out. Royce might have done his best to try to forget her again—as if that might have happened—if Ellie hadn't called. She'd cursed a blue streak, calling him every name in the book for not going after Merida. It seemed that, as far as commitment went, Merida might even be more screwed up than he was.

So he'd packed a bag and chased her. Again. This would be the last time. But he had a trump card to play now. He knew how she felt about him, and he had no problem using it to his advantage.

He sat in her living room—in the middle of the day, of all times—waiting for her to get home. The male who claimed to be her housekeeper had been easy to get rid of. One flash of his fangs and the wimp had taken off. That worked out well for both of them, because Royce would have had to kill the guy if he hadn't left. He didn't like the thought of Merida being alone, day after day, with him. Young guys like that only caused trouble.

The sound of the front door opening and closing echoed through the room, followed by the clack of high-heeled shoes on the shiny tile floor. A second later, Merida rounded the corner. "I thought I smelled vampire."

She looked better than he'd ever seen her, and he ached all over again. He was a goner, plain and simple. If she didn't see things his way, he didn't know what he'd do. It wouldn't be pretty, that much he could guarantee.

"Nice to see you, too," he murmured.

"What do you want?" Her voice held a little too much edge, her glare a little too much fire. He didn't buy the act for a second. But he didn't try to stop her, either. Not yet.

"Can't I check up on an old friend?"

"I've heard a similar line before. Didn't work that time, either." She turned and started back across the room. "You know the way out."

He let her get almost all the way to the door leading out of the room before he spoke. "If you love me, you won't walk away from me again."

She froze. He didn't need to see her face to know the internal dilemma going on inside her. If she kept walking, she'd lose. If she stayed, she'd be admitting weakness. For a second he expected her to go for broke and walk away, but she turned slowly back to him, one hand on her hip and the other balled into a fist at her side. "How dare you throw that in my face?"

He stood and walked to her, stopping a few feet from where she stood. "How dare you walk away from me without a goodbye again?"

She blinked, her gulp audible in the big room. "I did what was right for both of us."

"Bullshit."

"*Excuse me?*"

"You heard me." He shook his head and gave a humorless laugh. "You know how I feel about you. I told you. But you're so closed off you can't even see what a good thing we could have if you'd just let it happen."

"No strings. No labels. Remember?"

He remembered. Now he wished she'd forget. "I don't

want that."

"Well, I do."

He didn't think so. He just stared at her, searching her gaze, and a tear slipped down her cheek. "Don't do this, Royce. Please. I'm safe now. You don't have to protect me any more."

Protect her? What was she talking about? "I'm not following you, sweetheart."

"You said to me that you'd stay with me until you knew I was safe."

He closed his eyes briefly, fighting the equally strong urges to pull her into his arms and shake some sense into her. He drew a deep breath and opened his eyes, not moving from where he stood. "I didn't think you'd take it so literally. I never meant to push you away."

"You didn't?"

He shook his head. "No. And as far as I'm concerned, woman, you're a loose cannon. You're too impulsive. Never think of your own safety. I'm not sure you'll ever be truly safe."

She laughed at his comment, but at the same time a tear slipped down her cheek. "Really?"

"Yeah, so it looks like you're going to be stuck with me for a long time. Maybe forever. Until you curb your impulsive urges, you're going to have to deal with me being around."

She took a small step closer to him, blinking her eyes. "I can't change who I am. I'm afraid to tell you I'm always going to be a bit on the impulsive side."

"Forever?" he asked, finally letting himself go enough to smile.

She sniffled. "I'm afraid so."

He shook his head. "Then I guess you're just going to have to deal with me hanging around. You know. Just to make sure you're safe."

She ran to him and wrapped her arms around his neck. He smoothed her curls down with the palm of his hand. "What is it you want from me, Merida? Whatever you want, you can have it. I'll do anything for you. You know that, don't you?"

"What do you want?" he repeated when she didn't answer.

She pulled out of his arms and looked up at him with uncertain eyes. "More than you could ever give me."

"Tell me. You might be surprised."

She hesitated for only a second before blurting, "I want to tie you up, like you did with me."

He gulped. *Shit.* Whose *brilliant* idea had it been to offer her anything she wanted, anyway?

* * * * *

Merida looped a scarf around the headboard, securing Royce's arm above his head. His gaze followed her every move as she checked the knot before moving on to the other one. When she finished she scooted off the bed to admire her man—completely, beautifully naked, strapped to her wrought iron headboard like the best gift she'd ever received. She licked her lips in anticipation.

"Don't do that," Royce growled. She saw the intense arousal in his eyes, which set her mind at ease. She'd been afraid he'd say no, and after he'd agreed she'd been afraid he'd change his mind. Now she knew he wouldn't. She smiled.

"Get out of your clothes and come over here, will you?" he asked. She laughed at his demands.

"Who is in charge here?"

"You are. For now." He spoke the last two words with a distinct warning tone in his voice—one that sent quivers through her already soaked pussy. He'd already started planning his payback.

She couldn't wait.

But now, she intended to enjoy her few minutes of being the one in complete control. She'd learned she didn't mind giving over her control to him, at least in the sexual sense, but she liked the feeling of power that came with having a big, hard man tied to her bed, waiting to be pleased.

She lit one of the white candles on her bedside table, shaking the match out and dropping it onto the glass candle plate. Royce laughed. "Can the ambiance wait until next time? I've been without you too long. I feel like I'm going to explode."

She toed off her shoes and kicked them under the bed. "The candle isn't for atmosphere." She unzipped her sundress and shimmied out of it, letting it drop to the floor. Her panties and bra followed before she raised one leg on the bed and peeled off her stocking. Royce's breath hitched and she smiled to herself as she switched legs, slowly pulling the stocking down her leg. When both were off, she tossed them over her shoulder.

"Come here, beautiful," Royce told her. Her smile widened as she climbed into the bed and straddled his hips, rubbing her drenched pussy over the head of his rock-hard cock before settling onto his stomach. He groaned. "Tease."

"I seem to remember you teasing me not too long ago." She lifted the candle from its holder and held it over his chest.

"What are you doing?" he asked, his eyes dark with lust.

"Having a little fun." She tipped the candle, dribbling a line of hot wax over his chest.

He hissed, then moaned. "*Fuck.*"

"Soon," she promised, tipping the candle again and dotting his chest with the wax. He arched his hips against her, his cock sliding against her ass. "What do you want now, vampire?"

"Ride me," he begged. "Climb on top of me and let me fuck you. Now."

She set the candle back in the holder and leaned over, blowing it out with an exaggerated breath. She heard Royce's sharp intake of breath seconds before she heard the scarves snap. She turned her head toward him just in time to see him lunge up and reach for her. She tried to get off his lap, but he was too quick for her. He rolled her over and pinned her down beneath him on the mattress, his big body between her thighs and his cock against her slit. Her pussy dripped, fluids trailing down the insides of her thighs. She whimpered.

"Enough," Royce told her, his voice harsh. "I need to be inside you. Now."

He pushed his cock into her waiting cunt, all the way to the hilt in a single thrust. "I'm sorry, Merida, but after that display I'm not going to last long."

She smiled up at him even as she felt the stirrings of orgasm start in her belly. "That's okay. Neither am I."

He lifted her hips to adjust her position, causing his pelvic bone to grind against her mound. Her body convulsed in a fast, intense orgasm that left her gasping for breath. Royce's thrusts grew harsher, his breathing jagged, and his grip on her hips tightened. She wrapped her arms around his neck and buried her face against his shoulder, inhaling his scent. Why had she ever thought walking away would be a good idea? It made no sense now, lying in his arms, holding him the way she'd longed to do since she'd walked away from him a few weeks ago.

Royce shuddered and stiffened above her, her name escaping his lips on a groan as he came. After a few minutes, he rolled to his side, his fingertips circling her still-peaked nipples. "I'm sorry."

"For what?"

"For everything. For being an ass. I can't guarantee that it won't happen again, but I'll try."

She licked her lips and waited, wondering if he was saying what she thought he was saying. "Would you care to explain that a little more?"

He leaned close to her and breathed against her neck, his breath tickling her skin. "I...um. Hell, I don't even know where to begin. It's been four hundred years since I've had this discussion with anyone."

She smiled, but kept it to herself. Could it possibly be what she'd been hoping for? "Sometimes the best way is to just say it."

He nodded and muffled his face further into her neck. "Okay. You're right. Merida, I love you. I meant it the first time, and I mean it even more now."

"What was that?" she asked. "I couldn't understand you with your face shoved against my shoulder."

He heaved a sigh and looked up. "Witch."

She shrugged. "I'm tough when I have to be. Say it, mister, or you're going to have to find somewhere else to sleep."

"I love you, Merida." This time when he said it, he looked right into her eyes.

"I love you, too, you big idiot." She nipped his jaw, laughing when he did the same to her.

"Forever?" he asked.

"Duh." She leaned up and kissed him.

"Oh, I heard from Wil," she told him when she broke the kiss.

"Yeah, me too. He sent me a postcard from Seattle, of all places."

"That's what I got, too." Merida smiled.

"He hooked up with some busty blonde werewolf," Royce said. "That's not exactly hard to believe."

"He didn't mention anything about busty or blonde to me."

"I'm not surprised." Royce leaned in for a quick kiss. "He knows how jealous you get."

"Get real." She punched his arm. "So I guess he's happy now, huh?"

"For the moment. I wouldn't count on it lasting for too long, though. Wil isn't very good at commitment."

She laughed as Royce pulled her down for another kiss. "You never know," she told him in between kisses. "Look what happened with us."

"Yeah, amazing what a little *Aparasei* intervention will do."

"Hey. Whatever works," she told him before she rolled him onto his back. "Enough talk, Big Guy. I have other plans for you now."

"Make all the plans you want. You're going to be stuck with me for a long, long time."

She smiled down at him, the annoying pain in the ass she never wanted to let go.

Finally, after all this time, she had him right where she wanted him.

Epilogue

Royce leaned against a tree, watching Merida run free in the clearing up ahead. When they'd come to the small glen and she'd seen the mountain lion, her eyes had sparkled. He'd been ready to get out of the heat, but she'd wanted it so much. He couldn't bear to say no. The sun wasn't *that* bright, at least not under the cover of the trees with his dark sunglasses and baseball cap. And watching her run in cat form made up for any discomfort the sunlight caused.

He couldn't believe how easy it had been to accept her for what she truly was, once she'd proved to him how much she loved him. And how easily she'd wormed her way into his heart. He'd been closed off from his emotions for so long that it was taking some time to get used to, but she was getting through to him. Slowly, but she made a little more progress very day. He'd give her anything she wanted, as long as he got to spend the rest of his life with her. It had already been a year, and though the road could be rocky, he wouldn't trade any of it for the world. They fought well, and they made up even better. Every time.

When his usual wanderlust hit after being in Florida with her for too long, they left together. They rented out the house and spent six months traveling the world and had finally come back to the States—North Carolina this time. They'd come to relax after the whirlwind trip around the world, but so far hadn't managed much resting.

Merida started running toward him, her cat form

shifting as she did so, and by the time she reached him, she stood in front of him in all her naked glory. "Hey, handsome. Wanna have some fun?"

He shook his head. "Not in the middle of the woods, in the middle of the day."

"Danger is what's going to make it fun." She ran her hand along the hard ridge of his cock. "Please? I'll let you tie me to the bed when we get back to the hotel."

He laughed. She liked to be tied as much as he liked to tie her. "You'll let me tie you up anyway, and we both know it."

She sighed dramatically and shook her head. "Well, okay. We can leave if you insist. But if you flake out on me now we can't use the whips and chains when we get back to the room."

He immediately perked up, his cock tightening even more against the zipper of his pants. "Whips and chains? Really?"

"Well...I don't really have chains." She smiled. "Will handcuffs do?"

Enjoy this excerpt from
Just Another Night

© Copyright Elisa Adams 2002

Chapter 1

"I hope you know what you're doing," Erica said to the image reflected in the mirror in front of her. "Because if you aren't careful, you could get yourself into a lot of trouble."

She nervously tucked a strand of sleek blond hair behind her ear, swiped a third coat of double black mascara over her lashes, and blotted her deep red lipstick with a tissue from the box tucked under the vanity counter.

What she saw in the mirror scared her. She didn't even recognize herself. Her eyes, normally a clear blue, appeared almost navy with the dark eyeliner and glittery shadow she'd caked around them. She'd rouged her cheeks with red to accentuate her barely-there cheekbones, but she had a feeling she might have gone a little overboard.

The lips were the kicker. She had full lips to begin with, something she wasn't exactly crazy about showing off. But with the *notice-me* lipstick, she looked like she'd gotten collagen injections. According to the salesgirl at the makeup counter, this look was sure to attract some attention.

"This could be the best night of my life," she said to her reflection, testing a small smile, "Or the absolute worst."

Giving herself a final once-over, Erica decided she was as ready as she would ever be. She snapped off the bathroom light and walked into her hotel room on shaking legs. She'd barely made it to the bed when she found she had to sit down and get her bearings. This just wouldn't do. If she was going to pull this off tonight, she was going to have to get control of her raging insecurities. Other women did this sort of thing all the time. Why was she having so much trouble?

"Come on," Erica prodded herself, standing up and self-consciously tugging on the hem of her too-short red dress. She had the sudden urge to change into a pair of jeans and her favorite sweatshirt. Maybe then her body might relax.

This dress simply wasn't comfortable. It was sexy as hell, even she could tell that much, but comfort had obviously not been in the designer's mind when he created the fiery velvet concoction. But what choice did she have? She needed a come-hither dress tonight—it was the only way this was going to work. Men simply did not look at Erica Blake as a sexy siren. They never had, and they never would; at least not without a lot of help. Tonight she was going to do something about that.

The dress hugged Erica's curves in all the right places. The salesgirl at the boutique had told her she would have every male with a pulse beating a path to her door when she wore it. That was exactly what Erica was counting on. Only she didn't need every man on the planet. One would do just fine. Tall, dark, and sexy as all get out. Just for tonight, those were her only criteria.

She rubbed her hands up and down her arms vigorously, trying in vain to warm her chilled body. She'd come too far to chicken out now. She'd bought the dress, bathed in jasmine scented water, spent an hour on her hair and makeup, and even rented a pricey hotel room, one she could barely afford. She was bound and determined to do this, and it was going to happen tonight. Her friends thought she needed more excitement in her life, and she was going to get it, even if it killed her.

She needed sex. Dirty, anonymous sex with someone she'd never met before and would never see again. Incredible sex that she'd never forget. Tonight, she was going to get exactly what she needed.

The only thing missing from her plan was a ready and willing man, preferably an irresistibly sexy one. She hoped one of those would be easy to come by in the bar across the street. From what she'd heard about the place, finding a good man willing to spend the night with a woman was never a problem. Erica intended to put that theory to the test, if she could convince herself to actually take a step out of her hotel room, that is.

She wanted to do this. She really did. It had *nothing* to do with the fact that everyone thought she was dull. It had *nothing* to do with the fact that her first serious boyfriend had played her for a total fool. It had *nothing* to do with the fact that she'd never experienced good sex, not really.

Tonight was about Erica Blake figuring out who she was as a woman, who she could be if she let go of her silly inhibitions and tried something, or someone, new. Tonight was all about Erica. No one else mattered. She could be whoever she wanted to be, and who she wanted to be was a woman who actually felt alive. She would finally bury the aching emptiness she'd felt ever since Carl left, at least for tonight.

"It's now or never," Erica said. She felt a sudden rush of excitement. She grabbed her handbag and keys and hurried out the door before she could change her mind. Tonight would be a night to remember, she would make sure of it. Erica Blake was finally going to know what it meant to live.

* * * * *

Erica closed her eyes and took a deep, cleansing breath before she pulled open the heavy wooden door of the bar and stepped inside. The loud music, chatter of the customers, and cigarette smoke that hung in the air overwhelmed her, caused her nerve to slip more than a little.

She closed her eyes and breathed deeply. She could do this. It wasn't that hard. Millions of women did it all the time. She walked over to the bar and took a seat on one of the few empty stools.

Almost as soon as she sat down a short, balding man slid onto the seat next to her.

"Can I buy you a drink?"

"No, thank you." Erica forced herself to unclench her fists, which she had made into tight balls the second she heard his grating voice.

"Just one drink?"

He was definitely *not* the type of man she was interested in. Not tonight. Erica sighed and looked away. "I don't think so."

"Maybe we could dance, then." He took her hand in his sweaty one and tried to get her to stand up. She pulled her hand away and wiped her palm on her thigh. "Look, I'm not interested."

Maybe this wasn't the right kind of place to find the man of her fantasies. Maybe she should try somewhere a little less, well, busy, like the library or the grocery store. Maybe she'd be better off just turning around and going home.

"Why not?" He had the gall to look genuinely confused. "Are you waiting for someone?"

"Yes. I am." Erica couldn't have thought of a better excuse on her own. "Now if you'll pardon me…"

"I think I'll just stick around until he gets here." The man made himself comfortable on the stool next to Erica's. "Then if he doesn't show up you won't have to sit here alone."

"How kind of you." Erica rolled her eyes.

"My name's Trent." He held out his hand, which Erica absolutely refused to touch again.

"That's nice." Erica turned her head in the opposite direction and drummed her nails against the bar.

"What's your name?" He just couldn't take a hint.

"I'm involved with somebody."

"Well, he's not here now, is he?" Trent's oily smile gave her the creeps.

She was seriously considering scrapping her plan altogether when she saw him. She knew he was the right man by the way her heart thumped loudly against the wall of her chest and her pulse kicked into overdrive. He was sitting at the other end of the bar, toying with the label on the bottle of beer in front of him. He had to be the best looking man Erica had ever seen, and he seemed to be alone. Erica had found her perfect man. Now she just had to convince him they were destined to spend an incredible evening together in each other's arms.

"Actually, he is." She pointed to where her dream guy was sitting. "Thanks for keeping me company."

She flashed the jerk her biggest smile and walked across the room.

Absorbed only in the drink in front of him, he didn't look like he was waiting for anyone. That was a good sign. Mustering all the courage she could manage, Erica sauntered her way to the bar, or at least did the best she could on her four-inch heels, and slid onto the stool next to him. She ordered a red wine from the bartender, stealing sidelong glances at the Greek God on the next stool.

The man was sheer physical perfection. Just sitting next to him, Erica could feel electricity humming in the air around him. Her fingers itched to get tangled in his thick black hair, and she could just imagine what his strong hands would feel like running all over her body. His broad shoulders and muscled physique suggested someone who knew how to take care of himself. Erica liked that in a man. Now she just needed to get up the courage to talk to him.

"So what's a pretty lady like you doing in a place like this?" the man asked, catching her off guard. Lost in her own fantasies, she hadn't noticed that he'd been looking at her until he spoke.

"E-excuse me?" Erica fumbled for a sexy reply but unable to think of anything. When his dark gaze met hers, all thoughts were erased from her mind. She mentally berated herself for acting so inexperienced. This was *not* the way to catch a man.

"This just doesn't seem like your kind of place," he continued slowly, his piercing green eyes never leaving hers.

God, he just smoldered. Just a few sentences and the man had her damn near hypnotized.

"I come here all the time," she lied, hoping that he didn't notice. Fat chance. She was fumbling this whole thing badly, but she couldn't seem to help it. She was way out of her league, and she had the sinking feeling he knew it.

"Yeah, sure you do," the man said, his voice so deep and sexy Erica's legs turned to jelly. She was glad she was sitting down, or she might have embarrassed herself further by fainting at his feet.

"What's your name, sweetheart?" he asked. His fingers snaked out and brushed against the back of her hand. His touch sent little jolts of electricity through Erica's entire body.

"Carolyn." She recited the first name that popped into her head. It figured that it would be Carolyn. Her best friend, the woman who had convinced her to do this tonight. Carolyn would get a month's worth of laughs when she heard this story, and if Erica was ever brave enough to fess up about her embarrassing failure.

"Carolyn," the man echoed huskily, and Erica thought she caught a glimpse of humor in his voice. Could he tell she wasn't being truthful? Was she really that obvious? She looked down at her drink, unable to meet his knowing gaze any longer.

"What are you doing here, Carolyn? Are you looking for something in particular?" He hooked a finger under her chin and lifted her eyes back to his.

The heat, the blatant longing she found in his eyes bolstered her confidence.

"Yes, you," Erica said before she could stop herself.

The second the words were out of her mouth, she wished she could take them back. She just wasn't cut out to be a modern woman. Instead of sounding sexy and desirable, she'd only sounded pitifully ridiculous.

The man stared at her, mouth slightly agape, for what seemed like an eternity before he spoke again.

"Me?" he asked, looking genuinely surprised. "I don't know you, do I? I think I would have remembered a lady as beautiful as you."

Beautiful? No one had called Erica that before besides her own father. She'd been called conservative, classy, even pretty on the rare occasions that she took the time to dress up. She knew she wasn't hideous, but she certainly wasn't a fashion model, either. She couldn't describe herself as tall or short, fat or thin. She pretty much fell somewhere in the middle with everything. She was average, and on any other night she'd be happy to keep it that way.

But he thought she was beautiful. A slow smile crept across her lips at this man's words. Maybe this night would be all she imagined, after all.

"You don't know me." Erica wondered where her newfound courage had come from. "But do you want to?"

"Hell, yes," he answered, his hand making slow circles up Erica's arm. "Can I buy you another drink?"

"No, thanks," Erica said softly. She didn't want an alcohol-induced haze to ruin her memories of the evening. "One's enough for me."

He chuckled softly as Erica lifted the glass to her lips. She grimaced at the taste of the dark red liquid—she'd never been much of a drinker. After a few attempts at looking sophisticated, Erica finally gave up and gulped down the contents of the entire glass. Eyes watering, she set the glass on the bar in front of her and tried to look like she did this sort of thing all the time.

"You don't like wine, do you?" Her stranger picked up the wine glass and swirled the last drop of liquid around in the bottom. He lifted the glass to his own lips, right on Erica's lipstick mark, and drank the last bit. "That's too bad. It's a good wine. Definitely worth savoring."

"Really?" She hoped she didn't sound as clueless as she felt. Her experience with wine was limited to the jug grocery store variety.

"Really." He stared at the glass. "Definitely not what I expected here."

Erica couldn't help but wonder if he was talking about her or the wine.

"Well, Carolyn," he said smoothly. He raised her hand to his lips and kissed her knuckles gently. "You don't seem comfortable here. You want to go somewhere else?"

"I thought you'd never ask..."

About the author:

Born in Gloucester, Massachusetts, Elisa Adams has lived most of her life on the east coast. Formerly a nursing assistant and phlebotomist, writing has been a longtime hobby. Now a full time writer, she lives on the New Hampshire border with her husband and three children.

Elisa welcomes mail from readers. You can write to her c/o Ellora's Cave Publishing at 1056 Home Avenue, Akron OH 44310-3502.

Why an electronic book?

We live in the Information Age—an exciting time in the history of human civilization in which technology rules supreme and continues to progress in leaps and bounds every minute of every hour of every day. For a multitude of reasons, more and more avid literary fans are opting to purchase e-books instead of paperbacks. The question to those not yet initiated to the world of electronic reading is simply: *why?*

1. *Price.* An electronic title at Ellora's Cave Publishing and Cerridwen Press runs anywhere from 40-75% less than the cover price of the <u>exact same title</u> in paperback format. Why? Cold mathematics. It is less expensive to publish an e-book than it is to publish a paperback, so the savings are passed along to the consumer.

2. *Space.* Running out of room to house your paperback books? That is one worry you will never have with electronic novels. For a low one-time cost, you can purchase a handheld computer designed specifically for e-reading purposes. Many e-readers are larger than the average handheld, giving you plenty of screen room. Better yet, hundreds of titles can be stored within your new library—a single microchip. (Please note that Ellora's Cave and Cerridwen Press does not endorse any specific brands. You can check our website at www.ellorascave.com or

www.cerridwenpress.com for customer recommendations we make available to new consumers.)

3. *Mobility.* Because your new library now consists of only a microchip, your entire cache of books can be taken with you wherever you go.

4. *Personal preferences are accounted for.* Are the words you are currently reading too small? Too large? Too...**ANNOYING**? Paperback books cannot be modified according to personal preferences, but e-books can.

5. *Instant gratification.* Is it the middle of the night and all the bookstores are closed? Are you tired of waiting days—sometimes weeks—for online and offline bookstores to ship the novels you bought? Ellora's Cave Publishing sells instantaneous downloads 24 hours a day, 7 days a week, 365 days a year. Our e-book delivery system is 100% automated, meaning your order is filled as soon as you pay for it.

Those are a few of the top reasons why electronic novels are displacing paperbacks for many an avid reader. As always, Ellora's Cave and Cerridwen Press welcomes your questions and comments. We invite you to email us at service@ellorascave.com, service@cerridwenpress.com or write to us directly at: 1056 Home Ave. Akron OH 44310-3502.

NEED A MORE EXCITING
WAY TO PLAN YOUR DAY?

ELLORA'S
CAVEMEN

2006 CALENDAR

COMING THIS FALL

THE
ELLORA'S CAVE
LIBRARY

Stay up to date with Ellora's Cave Titles
in Print with our Quarterly Catalog.

To RECIEVE A CATALOG,
SEND AN EMAIL WITH YOUR NAME
AND MAILING ADDRESS TO:

CATALOG@ELLORASCAVE.COM

OR SEND A LETTER OR POSTCARD
WITH YOUR MAILING ADDRESS TO:

CATALOG REQUEST
c/o ELLORA'S CAVE PUBLISHING, INC.
1337 COMMERCE DRIVE #13
STOW, OH 44224

Discover for yourself why readers can't get enough of the multiple award-winning publisher Ellora's Cave. Whether you prefer e-books or paperbacks, be sure to visit EC on the web at www.ellorascave.com for an erotic reading experience that will leave you breathless.

www.ellorascave.com

Printed in the United States
57442LVS00001B/23